The Teacher's Assistant

A Lesson in Love

By

José F. Nodar

Northport Booksellers / Spring Farm NSW Australia

Publisher's Note: This is a work of fiction. Names, characters, places, and incidents are a product of the author's imagination. Locales and public names are sometimes used for atmospheric purposes. Any resemblance to actual people, living or dead, or to businesses, companies, events, institutions, or locales is completely coincidental.

Spring Farm NSW Australia / José F. Nodar First Edition

ISBN 978-1-7640642-5-5 – Paperback

ISBN 978-1-7640642-6-2 – E-pub

ISBN 978-1-7640642-7-9 – Audiobook

Table of Contents

For Miriam,

Anna,

Elizabeth,

Allison,

Mark,

Rachel

David,

and

Andrea.

You are always in my thoughts.

Late Enrolment

I should have known something was off when I saw the course code: Lit 401. I figured it was some kind of administrative mix-up. After all, I'd only meant to register for a general literature class to fill an elective requirement, not an upper-level seminar. I went back to the registrar to see if I could get out of the class, but it was too late to switch.

So, as I walked into the auditorium, I looked around and realised that moment I was in over my head. Unlike the usual mix of hoodie-clad first- and second-year students, the room was filled with students who looked older, seasoned. I hesitated before sliding into an open seat between two guys who appeared much older than me.

I turned to my left and offered a friendly nod to the guy in glasses with a tweed blazer. "Hey, I'm Ethan Carter."

He glanced at me before offering a brief smile. "Yeah, hi. I'm James Broughton. And unless you're some kind of literary prodigy, I think you look too young for this class."

"I am 22," I answered.

The guy on my right, a bearded man in his late twenties, chuckled. "A babe in the woods. I agree with James. Name's Mark Stevens. Are you sure you're in the right place, kid? This is Shakespeare and the Scandal of Power. This is a fourth-year student seminar."

I swallowed. "Yeah, I enrolled by mistake. I didn't realise it was an upper-level course until it was too late to switch. I tried to change to another class but could not get out of it, so I thought I'd give it a shot."

Mark shrugged. "Well, better hold on to your pantyhose, Ethan. I hear it's a tough one."

"Professor Sinclair's supposed to be brilliant, though. Have either of you taken a class with her before?" James added.

Mark shook his head. "Nope. But from what I've heard, she's intense. Apparently, she can make even the lectures sound dangerous."

I laughed. "Dangerous Shakespeare? Sounds like my kind of thing."

Before James or Mark could respond, the room fell silent as the door at the front of the lecture hall swung open. In walked Professor Olivia Sinclair.

I swear, for a moment, my entire world stopped.

She was unlike any professor I'd ever seen.

She looked to be in her early thirties with long, dark hair that cascaded past her shoulders, framing a face that I could only describe as devastatingly captivating with beautiful green eyes. She wore a tailored charcoal blazer over a silk blouse, paired with a pencil skirt, and when she moved, it was with the kind of effortless confidence that made every eye in the room follow her. Well, at least mine did.

"Good afternoon, class," she said, setting her satchel on the desk.

"Welcome to Shakespeare and the Scandal of Power. If you thought this would be just another literature course, I assure you, you're mistaken. Shakespeare was not a playwright for the faint of heart. His works are riddled with ambition, betrayal, and seduction."

I was like a deer looking at the headlights – I was transfixed.

She began speaking and weaving tales of corruption and desire from the Bard's pages. I hung on every word. Then, as if sensing my gaze, she looked straight at me.

Just for a second, her piercing green eyes locked onto mine. My breath hitched. And then, as quickly as it happened, she moved on.

I looked at both James and Mark, and all they did was take notes, and as the lecture continued, my mind was stuck in that fleeting moment. I was in for one hell of a semester.

2

The Coffee Incident

Keeping up with Lit 401 was like running a marathon with two gorillas holding me down at the same time. The readings were dense; the discussions felt at times way over my head, and I was barely holding my own. But I couldn't, no, I wouldn't withdraw. Not when Professor Sinclair's lectures were the highlight of my week.

I was lucky enough to hook up with James and Mark by becoming their roommate, and I sought their help. They'd offer the occasional bite-sized idea or suggestion, but since they were always wrapped up in reading and studying, it was clear I was pretty much on my own.

One afternoon, after class, I wandered into the local coffee shop near the university, craving a caffeine boost. As I stepped inside, I froze. There, standing in front of me, with her back to me, waiting for her coffee, was Professor Sinclair.

I swallowed hard and did my best to act casual. Which, apparently, meant standing way too close behind her in line. Close enough to catch a whiff of her perfume, something fruity and subtly floral. Close enough to make this officially weird.

Before I could step back, she spun, and — "Oh!" she gasps as her coffee flew straight onto my shirt.

Hot. Scalding. Liquid. Right. On my brand-new pullover shirt.

"Ah! Oh—uh—hot! Coffee! Me—shirt—ow!" I babble, waving my hands around like a malfunctioning windmill.

Professor Sinclair's eyes widened. "Oh, my goodness! I am so sorry! Are you all, right?"

"Yes! No! I mean, goodness, which is hot! But fine! Probably!" I stammer, mentally kicking myself for forgetting how to speak like a normal human being.

She pressed a handful of napkins against my chest, which only made me more flustered. "Here, let me—oh, you're soaked. I really am sorry."

"It's fine. Happens all the time," I lied, as if getting doused in coffee by a stunning professor was a routine occurrence in my life.

She chuckled, a soft, amused sound. "I doubt that." She glanced at the barista. "Another coffee, please. And one for him, on me."

"Oh, you don't have to."

"Consider it my apology," she says smoothly.

I nodded, still standing there awkwardly, still holding the damp napkins. "Cool. Cool, yeah. Thanks."

She smiled. "You're in my class, right? Ethan, isn't it?"

She knew my name.

"Yeah, that's me," I finally managed, though my voice cracked slightly. "Ethan Carter. The, uh, designated class coffee casualty."

She laughs with her rich and warming tone. "I'll have to make a note of that in my roster. Ethan Carter: loves Shakespeare, occasional coffee victim."

I groan, but I couldn't help grinning. "Great. Immortalised in class history."

She shook her head, amusement dancing in her eyes. "Well, Ethan Carter, since I've officially ruined your afternoon, let me at least offer you a seat while we wait for our drinks."

I blinked. "Oh. Yeah, sure! That'd be—cool. Totally cool."

Like the proper gentleman my father taught me, I pulled her chair first, and she sat, and I slid in the chair across from her.

"So, while we wait for our coffee, Ethan. Tell me about yourself."

I spend the next five minutes going over my family tree and can't seem to stop talking, which amuses Olivia. When the coffee arrives, Olivia looks at me, smiles and says: "I once again wish to apologise for ruining your shirt. Let me know if it does not clean, and I will be more than happy to pay you for a new one."

"Oh, I am sure it will clean just fine. Professor Sinclair, may I ask you a personal question?"

Olivia is taken aback a bit, but nods.

"What is the lovely perfume you are wearing?"

With a smile, Oliva simply answers: "It is my favourite. It is called Dior J'adore, and I love wearing it because it has a flowery and fruity smell to it. I wear it all the time. Why do you ask Ethan?"

"I just wonder. It is quite becoming of you."

"Why thank you. I rarely receive a compliment for it. Ethan, it's my turn to ask you a question. May I?"

"Of course," I answer.

"How do you feel you are doing with my class? Do you feel you could become my teacher's assistant, my TA? Or am I asking too much of you so early in the piece?"

"No, no, I am fine, and yes, I would love to be your assistant if you feel I am ready. Besides, James and Mark are the ones asking for help."

Olivia gives me a smile, and I start to melt.

"Well, let me start the paperwork on getting you some credentials, and if you need any help, please do not hesitate to ask me. OK?"

"Sure. I will," I quickly answer, smiling like an idiot.

"Now, I must be going. I have a class to prepare for. See you in class tomorrow."

"Sure. I'll be there," I say as Olivia gets up and walks out of the coffee shop, leaving me with the unmistakable feeling that– for the first time since enrolling in Lit 401– I might've just died and gone to heaven. Even if it came at the cost of a ruined shirt and whatever dignity I had left.

3

The After-Hours Meeting

The next day, I slumped into my usual seat beside James and Mark in one of the study rooms, rubbing my temples. "Guys, this assignment. I am confused. I just do not get it. I have written something, but I am not sure I have it down correctly. It's like Professor Sinclair expects us to channel Shakespeare himself."

James smirked. "You're not the only one struggling. But at least you've got an edge."

"What? How?" I frowned.

Mark chuckled. "You've got an in with the professor. You bumped into her at a coffee shop. You sat with her for a while. Had a coffee, man. Take advantage of it, man. Go to her for help. After office hours."

I groaned. "You make it sound so easy."

James adds: "Send her an email and say you are desperate and need help. Do it now."

I open my laptop and shot a quick email to Professor Sinclair's office.

"See, that was easy. I bet she answers you right away."

"Cut it out, Mark. She is probably busy and will not even answer the email for a day or two."

Then I hear the familiar notification ping, and I look and there it was. A response from her.

James notices my stupefied face and asks.

"Was that her?"

"Yes," I answer. "She says to come over this evening after hours."

"Man, oh man, you are in like flint."

I give them both a look and leave them behind to gather my thoughts before going to the office, and I hear them laughing as I step out of the study room.

But I had no choice. That evening, I found myself outside Professor Sinclair's office, knocking hesitantly.

"Come in," she called.

I stepped inside; my voice awkward. "Uh, hi, Professor Sinclair. It's me. Ethan."

She smiled knowingly. "Ethan Carter, the class coffee casualty. What can I do for you?"

I sigh. "I do not know what I'm doing with this paper. Thanks for meeting with me about the literature paper."

She nodded. "Of course. Take a seat. You mentioned in your email you were struggling with the concepts?"

"Yeah, I realise I am supposed to be your TA, but I keep going in circles trying to connect the stream-of-consciousness technique in his writing, but it feels forced."

Oliva smiles at me and adds: "Let me see what you have written so far, Ethan."

I hand her my paper.

Olivia leans forward slightly. "That's actually an intriguing angle. What made you draw that parallel?"

"Well," I say as I shift in my seat, meeting her eyes with growing confidence, "It's the way both capture the rush of thoughts and fragments of daily life. The constant flow of..." I stop, noticing her smile and ask: "What?"

"Nothing. It's just refreshing to see someone get genuinely excited about literature. Most students treat it like a chore."

"I guess I'm not most students." I give the bookshelves behind Olivia a quick glance to play it cool!

"Is that the complete works of Borges? The Aleph is one of my favourites."

Olivia's eyes lit up. "You've read Borges? For fun?"

"I have a thing for magical realism. And brilliant people who can discuss it."

Olivia felt her cheeks warm slightly. She straightened in her chair, maintaining her professional demeanour despite the flutter in her stomach. "Well, Ethan, your literary taste is surprisingly sophisticated."

"Yeah, at least when we're discussing books outside of class?"

Sarah hesitated for a moment, then smiles. "Speaking of books outside of class, have you read any Guy Gavriel Kay?"

The conversation shifted away from his paper, their shared enthusiasm for literature breaking down the formal barriers between them, though both carefully maintained that delicate line between friendly and too friendly.

Then the subject turned to science fiction and fantasy novels.

"Wait, wait, tell me you've read 'Cryptic Spaces Book 1: Foresight' by Deen Ferrell," Olivia says, eyes alight.

"Are you kidding?" I gasp. "That book made me terrified of going to the barbershop for a week. It made me see patterns where there were no patterns."

She laughed. "I'll never look at my salon the same way again."

"Okay, but have you read Greg Mutton's 'Reunion: Chronicle of the 12th Realm' series; it has it all. Wealth, success, freedom, and some fancy space battles."

Olivia's eyes widened.

"Alright, I must read that. But you must promise me you'll check out J. F. Nodar's The Time Bus."

"Sounds amazing already. Do they wield laser watches?"

"Even better. They travel back in time and meet special people. I am not telling. You'll love it."

The awkward tension eased as we continued to debate different novels, exchanged recommendations, and laughed over guilty pleasure reads.

"OK, let me read the paper a bit more, and I will email you some notes, OK?"

"That would be great Oli..., I mean Professor Sinclair," and I stand and leave her office.

During the conversation, I slipped in an Olivia or two, and she did not correct me, and for the first time since enrolling, Lit 401 didn't feel impossible. And Professor Sinclair, Olivia? Maybe not as intimidating as I'd thought.

That's Cute Man

A couple of weeks had passed since I went to Professor Sinclair's office after hours, and James and Mark have not stopped pushing me to do a ridiculous bet. They swore up and down that I, Ethan Carter, would never have the guts to ask Olivia Sinclair out. Olivia wasn't just another girl in our college, she was Professor Sinclair, our Lit professor. Smart, attractive, witty, and way out of my league, but for some reason, I had convinced myself that there had been a few moments between us. A shared glance, a smirk at my sarcastic comments in class, an extra second of eye contact when she handed back an essay. Our conversation in her office when we discussed novels. There was something there. Right?

Maybe it was all in my head. Actually, it was definitely in my head. But that hadn't stopped me from letting James and Mark get into my head, too.

"You won't do it," James had said, leaning back against the couch in the student hall, arms crossed. "You talk a big game, but you don't have the balls."

Mark, ever the instigator, had grinned and nodded. "He's right, man. You keep saying she likes you, but we both know that if it ever came down to it, you'd choke. No way you're asking her out."

"Why do I even need to ask her out?" I shot back. "Maybe she should ask me out."

James burst out laughing. "Oh yeah, sure, because that happens all the time, professors sweeping their barely passing students off their feet."

"Hey, I'm not barely passing."

Mark tilted his head. "I mean, it's not a strong A either."

It was a losing battle, and I knew it. I should've just shut up and let it go, but James and Mark had this way of pushing my buttons. And after a couple of beers, I felt invincible. Or maybe just reckless.

"Fine," I blurted out. "I'll do it."

James and Mark looked at each other, then back at me, waiting. "Do what, exactly?" James asked, raising an eyebrow.

I straightened my shoulders. "I'll ask Professor Sinclair out."

Mark grinned like a man who had just found a new form of entertainment. "You're actually serious?"

"Dead serious."

James smirked. "And when are you planning on doing this?"

I thought for a second. "Tomorrow. After class."

Mark whistled. "Oh, this is going to be good."

The next morning, I woke up to the worst hangover of my life and the sinking realisation that I had made a very, very stupid decision. But James and Mark remembered everything, and they were not about to let me back out.

"Big day today," Mark announced, slapping me on the back as we headed to class.

James nodded. "You ready?"

"No," I grumbled.

James shrugged. "Doesn't matter."

And with that, they herded me into the lecture hall.

Professor Sinclair was already at the front of the class, writing something on the board when we walked in. She turned slightly, her sharp green eyes scanning the room, before landing on me for a brief second. She gave a small, almost imperceptible smirk before continuing to write.

Great. Even that felt like a mind game. Was she expecting me to say something today? Did she know? Or was I just hallucinating signs that weren't there?

Class dragged. Normally, I loved her lectures, but today, I couldn't focus on a single word. My pulse was hammering, and every time I thought about what I was about to do, my palms got clammy. James and Mark, of course, were loving every second of my suffering, exchanging knowing glances and barely holding back laughter.

Finally, the class ended, and students began shuffling out. James and Mark lingered by the door, watching, waiting. I took a deep breath, wiped my sweaty hands on my jeans, and stood up.

I walked to the front of the room, where Professor Sinclair was packing up her things. My heart was pounding, but there was no turning back now.

She glanced up as I approached. "Ethan."

Her voice was smooth, unreadable.

I cleared my throat. "Hey, Professor Sinclair."

She raised an eyebrow. "Something on your mind?"

Okay. This was it. No backing down. No chickening out.

I took another deep breath. "I was wondering if you'd like to go to dinner with me."

There was a pause. An exceedingly long pause.

Then she smirked. Not an amused smirk, not a cruel one either—just... something else. Something I couldn't quite read.

"That's cute," she said.

And then she just walked out.

I stood there, absolutely stunned, as James and Mark lost their minds standing by the door.

James was practically wheezing. "Dude, she actually said 'That's cute, man.' And then just left!"

Mark wiped away the fake tears. "That was brutal. Like, I actually felt pain for you, man."

I turned around slowly, my dignity hanging on by a thread. "What the hell does that even mean? 'That's cute'?"

Mark grinned. "It means she thinks you're an adorable little idiot."

James nodded solemnly. "Like a puppy trying to fight a Great Dane. It's sweet, but also, you know, doomed."

I groaned and ran a hand through my hair. "I thought she was into me! She enjoyed our conversation about science fiction and fantasy novels. She makes eye contact..."

James snorted. "She also makes eye contact with roadkill, Ethan."

Mark patted my shoulder. "Look, there are only two explanations. One: she was actually flattered but knew it was inappropriate, so she let you down gently. Or two—"

James cut in, smirking. "She thinks you're an idiot and enjoyed watching you crash and burn."

I groaned again. "Okay, but the smile? She smirked when she said it!"

Mark's face lit up. "Oh, maybe she wanted to see if you'd actually go through with it. Like, she's been grading your essays. She knows your brain cells are limited, and she thought, 'Let's see if he's really this dumb.'"

James grinned. "And congrats, my man. You are."

I pointed a finger at both of them. "You two made me do this. You hyped me up! If anything, this is your fault."

Mark shrugged. "Yeah, but we didn't just ask out Professor Sinclair. That was you."

James grinned. "And that's cute."

They both lost it again. I sighed, staring at the door Olivia had walked out of.

Maybe I'd drop her class. Or maybe I'd just never speak again.

5

Library Shenanigans

I walk through the towering wooden doors of the university's library, looking for a spot to work. "It is a beautiful library," I thought to myself as I sat down and placed my laptop on the table amongst all the books I had already retrieved to do my research.

I could smell the scent of old books around me, and I inhale deeply, as I sense that unmistakable library smell. A vanilla-like lignin compound released by aging paper, creating a sweet mustiness that feels almost edible.

While some of the older books carry some traces of their past readers, the newer ones contribute their fresh ink, binding glue, and crisp paper that hasn't yet mellowed with time.

I look around at the Gothic revival architecture that looms overhead, its ribbed vaults and stained-glass windows casting a scholarly glow across the space. I make my way through the main reading room, weaving past rows of oak study carrels and ancient card catalogues converted to decoration, until I find a spot to claim as my own. I spread out my books, some lying open while others are stacked in precarious towers. My laptop screen glows softly among the paper chaos, and a half-empty coffee cup sits dangerously close to what looks like a first edition. Even with the coffee, my eyes are feeling heavy and tired after a few hours of research.

I continue to scribble notes as I hunched over one particularly massive tome.

Desperate to redeem myself, I look at my watch and decide to spend another two hours buried in research, determined to ace my next paper. If I couldn't impress her with charm, maybe I could with intelligence. I was halfway through a stack of books on feminism and 18th-century poetry when exhaustion won.

Scrawled across my notes were passages like, "I am no bird; and no net ensnares me: I am a free human being with an independent will." (Charlotte Brontë, Jane Eyre). Another page had scribbled underlines on Mary Wollstonecraft's A Vindication of the Rights of Woman, especially the part about men keeping women in a state of ignorance as control.

I woke to soft laughter.

"Well, well, look at you," Professor Sinclair cooed, standing over me. "Drool-covered notes, tragic posture, and a desperate attempt at impressing me through literature?"

I groaned, wiping my face. "I'm just trying to..."

"Redeem yourself?" She smirked. "Why Ethan Carter, I appreciate the effort, but quoting Wollstonecraft and Brontë will not win you any favours." She glanced at another open book and grinned. "And The Rape of the Lock? Satirical poetry on female vanity? Brave choice."

I blinked. "Would reading The Second Sex by Simone de Beauvoir have been a better move?"

She grinned. "That would have been dangerously predictable."

I sighed, rubbing my temples. "Would it help if I brought you coffee and admitted I'm an idiot?"

Professor Sinclair tilted her head playfully. "It would be a start."

She leaned down, her voice lower now. "You know, Ethan, if you wanted my attention, there were easier ways than drowning in feminist literature. Though, I have to say the effort is charming."

I smirked, feeling a flicker of hope. "So, is that a compliment?"

She tapped a manicured finger against my notes. "It's a, maybe."

"Well then," I grinned, "I'll just have to keep trying."

"Why Ethan, I believe you are flirting with me. Are you trying to get me in trouble?"

I opened my mouth, but nothing came out. My brain short-circuited.

Was she joking?

Testing me?

The idea of getting her in trouble was ridiculous, since she was the one with all the power here. But the way she said it, the teasing lilt in her voice, the slight arch of her brow...

My throat went dry. "Uh, I mean..."

She smirked. "Oh, you poor little thing. I've truly broken you, haven't I?"

I let out a nervous laugh, rubbing the back of my neck. "A little bit, yeah."

Her eyes lingered on me for a second too long.

"Good and by the way, when we are alone, you can call me Olivia, OK?"

And with that, she turned on her heel and walked away, leaving me utterly, hopelessly, and deliciously confused.

6

The Almost Date

I lingered behind in the library long after Professor Olivia had walked out, her heels clicking against the polished floor and echoing in my ears even after the sound had disappeared. She hadn't meant to embarrass me—at least; I didn't think she had—but the way she'd smiled just before leaving, that half-smirk, half-kindness thing she did, made my stomach twist in all kinds of ways. She had complimented my analysis, said it was "surprisingly nuanced" for someone who usually half-sleeps through lectures. The words had landed somewhere between a compliment and a roast, and I hadn't quite recovered by the time she slung her coat over her arm and walked away.

"Surprisingly nuanced," I muttered to myself, finally gathering my notes into my backpack.

I paused, letting my hands rest on the cool surface of the table. The scent of old books and printer ink clung to the air, and for a few moments, I just sat there, letting everything settle. The flickering overhead light buzzed faintly above me, and the library, nearly empty now, felt like a world removed from time.

I needed to go. My dorm wasn't far, but I didn't want to leave just yet. Something about the quiet and the embarrassment still warming my cheeks made me want to stall. I wandered toward the exit, glancing at the bulletin board pinned full of flyers and ads: tutoring offers, book sales, club meetings, and—Win a Dinner for Two at Marcelli's – Enter Now!

My eyes snagged on the glossy cardstock.

The flyer was taped just below the student union logo, almost too neat to be real. I stepped closer, reading the fine print. Marcelli's. That was the place Professor Olivia had mentioned once in passing during a lecture—something about their risotto being "an actual reason to believe in the concept of joy." I'd never even seen the place in person. Too fancy for a broke undergraduate who lived on microwave ramen and vending machine pretzels.

The contest was simple: submit a brief paragraph on what "shared meals" mean in an academic community. A paragraph? I'd just written three pages for Professor Olivia about discourse in post-modern literary spaces. A paragraph was child's play. And for a chance at dinner at Marcelli's? I didn't even think and quickly took a photo of the QR code, pulled out my phone, and started typing.

"In the academic world, shared meals represent more than sustenance. They are an unspoken extension of the classroom, a moment where hierarchies soften, ideas flow freely, and connections deepen beyond whiteboards and textbooks."

Corny?

Maybe.

But I hit submit before I could overthink it.

If by some cosmic joke I actually won, I'd use it as an excuse—a thank-you dinner, nothing more. Just a casual gesture of gratitude for all her guidance this semester. I wouldn't even call it a date. Probably.

I walked back to my dorm, trying to forget I'd entered at all.

Two days passed.

I had almost forgotten about the contest by then.

Papers, classes, and my constantly crashing laptop took up enough mental space. I was halfway through reheating leftovers in the common kitchen when I got the email.

Subject: Congratulations! You've won the Marcelli's Gift Card!

I blinked at my screen.

At first, I thought it was spam.

Then I saw the university's logo at the bottom and the event coordinator's signature.

I laughed aloud. "No freaking way."

"What?" My roommate, James, called aloud.

"I just won a three-hundred-dollar gift card for dinner at Marcelli's."

"No freaking way." He echoed me exactly. "Wait, how? What did you do?"

"Wrote a few sentences about food and academics."

James raised an eyebrow. "And what, you gonna take me out on a fancy dinner date now?"

"Tempting," I said, smirking. "But I have someone else in mind."

James's eyes widened. "Oh. Her. You're finally doing it."

I looked down at the email again. My stomach did a nervous twist. "I mean, well, maybe. Sort of."

It took me another full day and an entire rejected draft of an email before I decided to ask her in person.

Office hours were quiet.

Only two students ahead of me, and neither stayed long. When I stepped into her small, book-filled office, Olivia looked up and gave me that same unreadable smile. Not mocking, not cold, but something in between "I know what you're up to" and "let's see what happens."

"Ethan," she said. "Back already?"

"I, yeah. Quick thing. I promise it's not about Chaucer."

She closed the book she was annotating and leaned back in her chair, eyes expectant.

I held up my phone, showing her the email. "So, I won this gift card at Marcelli's. Dinner for two."

Her eyebrows rose just a little. "Impressive."

"I figured since you recommended the place and since you've helped me a lot this semester, it might be nice to use it as a kind of thank-you. You know. Dinner. Just, uh, nothing formal. Casual. Appreciation. For all your time mentoring me."

I winced inwardly. I sounded like a TED Talk speaker having a stroke.

To her credit, Olivia didn't laugh. She tilted her head slightly, considering me. There was a long pause before she finally said, "That's very thoughtful of you."

I swallowed. "So, would you want to go?"

"I will," she said. "But I'll meet you there. I assume you're capable of making a reservation?"

"Totally. Yeah. Absolutely."

"Good." She smiled, and this time, it wasn't unreadable. "Then it's a date."

My brain short-circuited for a half second.

Or did she just say that casually?

Was it a figure of speech?

"Then it's a date."

That was what she said.

Was this an almost date?

I wasn't sure.

But I left her office with my heart thumping like I'd just sprinted across campus.

7

Friday Night at Marcelli's

I got there early, wearing the best button-up shirt I owned, which wasn't saying much. It was navy, slightly wrinkled despite my desperate ironing attempt, and just snug enough to make me uncomfortably aware of every breath I took. I kept checking my phone, running over what I'd say when she arrived. Something witty. Something light. Something not painfully awkward.

I must've scrolled through the same three apps about ten times. Eventually, I texted James:

She's not here yet. I'm going to combust.

He shot back instantly.

Be cool, Romeo. Don't spill anything on yourself.

As if he'd summoned her with that text, I looked up and there she was.

Professor Olivia Sinclair walked through the door like a slow, impossibly cinematic moment. She looked smashing.

That's the only word my dumb brain could come up with.

Smashing.

Her black dress was simple but elegant, ending just below her knees. She wore her hair down, loosely curled, like she hadn't even tried, but somehow still looked effortlessly perfect. A silver necklace caught the soft lighting and glinted every time she moved. When her eyes met mine, there was this quiet, amused confidence in them that made me forget how to breathe for a second.

I stood up too fast. My chair made this horrible screech against the floor, loud enough to make a couple at the next table flinch. Olivia arched one perfect eyebrow and smiled like she was already halfway to laughing at me.

"Are you okay over there?" she asked, voice warm and teasing.

"Fine! Totally fine," I said way too loud. "Just excited to see you."

Nice save, Ethan. Real smooth.

She laughed softly and made her way across the room, following the waiter to our table. I tried to pull out her chair and ended up yanking it way too far. She almost missed it but slid in gracefully, like nothing had gone wrong.

I sat down, flustered, already a little sweaty. Not ideal.

"You didn't have to dress up," she said, eyeing my shirt.

I ran a hand down my chest awkwardly. "I thought I'd, uh, try to match the ambiance."

"Well," she said, "you're definitely bringing something to the ambiance."

I couldn't tell if that was a compliment or a light jab, but it made me grin, anyway.

When the waiter came back, I reached for the menu and knocked my water glass. It didn't tip completely, but a solid splash landed right on my sleeve.

"Wow," I muttered, grabbing a napkin and trying to dab the water off.

She watched me with that same spark in her eye, like she was amused in the best possible way.

"Don't worry. Happens to the best of us."

"Does it?" I glanced up.

"No. But it's a nice thing to say."

I chuckled; grateful she wasn't even slightly annoyed.

Actually, she looked relaxed. Maybe even entertained.

We ordered.

Risotto for me, mushroom ravioli for her, and I tried to ease into conversation. But I was still too aware of myself. Every move I made felt exaggerated. I reached for the breadbasket and dropped a roll. I tried to pass her the butter and fumbled it like a live grenade. At one point, I called her professor instead of Olivia and immediately wanted to dig a hole and disappear into it.

"Old habits," I mumbled, cheeks burning.

"Understandable," she said. "But tonight, just Olivia."

"Right. Olivia. Of course."

I started repeating her name in my head like a chant, trying to keep myself from doing something else stupid which, of course, didn't work. I tried to say something clever about the décor, something about the minimalist lighting and abstract paintings, and right in the middle of it, I dropped my fork into my risotto. It made the saddest little slop noise.

I stared at it like it had betrayed me.

She laughed not mockingly, not even close. It was soft and almost fond, like she was watching someone try to do a magic trick with oven mitts on.

"You okay?" she asked, sipping her wine.

"Honestly? I'm hanging by a thread here."

"At least you're honest."

There was a brief pause while I picked up my fork again, trying to pretend like I still had some dignity left.

"You know," she said, tilting her head, "you're much more charming like this than when you're trying to impress me."

I blinked. "Wait? What? This is charming?"

"Absolutely. You're a walking disaster, but somehow it works."

I exhaled a laugh, feeling some of the nervous weight finally lift. "Thanks, I think?"

From there, the conversation got easier. Once I stopped trying so hard to be suave, which clearly wasn't in my toolkit, I started to just be me. We talked about books, sure, but also music, embarrassing travel stories (I told her about the time I fell asleep on a bus and ended up two towns over), and even her cat, who apparently hated every plant she brought into her apartment.

She was still technically my professor, yeah, but out here, away from campus and classrooms, she felt more like herself.

Witty.

Sharp.

Funny.

And when she talked, she made you feel like nothing else mattered but the conversation in that moment.

Dessert came, and I managed to eat it without incident, a small but proud victory. We lingered over coffee, both of us not quite ready to leave.

I still couldn't believe this was happening. A "not-a-date-but-kind-of-a-date" with Olivia Sinclair. And somehow, despite every fumble, every awkward moment, she was still smiling at me.

"You know," she said, glancing at her watch, "I was expecting this to be a lovely but very awkward evening."

"Well, you weren't wrong."

"True," she laughed. "But I didn't expect it to be quite so endearing."

There was a pause then. The kind that hung heavy with something unsaid.

"I meant what I said earlier," I said, leaning forward just a little. "About this not just being a thank-you dinner."

Her expression softened. "I know."

"I don't want to overstep, but I enjoy talking to you. I enjoy being around you."

She didn't look away. She just studied me for a moment, then nodded. "You're not overstepping. But this..." she gestured between us, "is complicated. I'm still your professor."

"For another six weeks."

She arched a brow. "Not that you're counting."

"Oh, I'm counting," I said, grinning before I could stop myself.

She smirked and swirled the last of her coffee in her cup. "You're persistent."

"And patient."

"And hopelessly awkward."

"Still somehow endearing?"

She chuckled. "Still somehow endearing."

Outside, the air was cool and quiet. We stood near the valet stand, the buzz of the city muffled under the night sky. Her car hadn't pulled up yet, and I wasn't in any hurry to say goodbye.

"You know," she said, glancing sideways at me, "if you keep fumbling like that, you might actually charm your way into real trouble."

"I've always been a fan of productive chaos."

She laughed again, tilting her head just slightly, her hair falling over one shoulder in that way that made my stomach turn into warm static.

"Well, Ethan, it was a lovely evening."

"I agree."

"But please no more thank-you dinners," she added, her voice teasing, her eyes sparkling. "Next time, you'll have to come up with a new excuse."

My heart thudded. "Challenge accepted."

Her car pulled up. She didn't hug me, didn't lean in, didn't make any grand gesture—just gave me one of those knowing smiles that made me feel like she knew. Like maybe she'd been just as curious about tonight as I had.

As she got in and the door shut, I stood there for a long moment, watching her drive away, already replaying everything in my head.

Every fumble.

Every smile.

And somehow, despite it all, maybe even because of it, I felt like I'd just had one of the best nights of my life.

And maybe it wasn't the last one.

8

Charming Interruption

I was still somewhere between asleep and comatose when I felt the unmistakable pressure of two full-grown human beings hovering in my personal space.

"Ethan. Ethan."

"Wake up, Romeo."

My eyes cracked open to see James and Mark leaning over me, practically nose-to-nose like twin gargoyles. James looked curious; Mark looked smug. Neither had the decency to wait for me to actually wake up before launching the ambush.

"Jesus," I muttered, rolling away and dragging the covers over my head. "Is it a crime to sleep in after a possibly life-altering dinner?"

James yanked the blanket back. "You got home at midnight, and you've been smiling in your sleep like a Disney princess. Spill it."

"I need coffee first," I croaked.

"You can sip while you talk," Mark said, already moving toward the kitchen. "We're making breakfast. Scrambled eggs and interrogation."

I groaned, sat up, and shuffled out of bed like a zombie doing a walk of shame. My shirt was still draped over my desk chair, crumpled and vaguely smelling like risotto and nerves. As I poured myself a mug of coffee, James, and Mark took their seats like this was a formal debriefing.

"So?" James said, hands steepled. "Was it awkward?"

"Yes," I admitted, then sipped. "But the good kind. The kind where she laughs at your clumsiness instead of calling security."

Mark whistled. "So, it went well."

"I think so," I said, leaning against the counter. "I spilled water on myself. Called her 'Professor.' Dropped my fork into my risotto. You know, standard charm offensive."

James cracked up. "You're such a walking disaster."

"Apparently that's endearing now," I said, shrugging.

Mark raised an eyebrow. "And she stayed through all that?"

"Not only stayed," I said, "she smiled through the whole thing. Laughed. Teased me. She told me I was more charming when I wasn't trying so hard."

James slapped the table. "She likes you, man."

I didn't respond right away.

I didn't know how to explain the weird mixture of lightness and tension that sat in my chest. It wasn't just a fun dinner. Something had shifted. But there was also a wall between us.

A six-week-tall wall.

"She said it's complicated," I whispered. "That she's still my professor."

James nodded, more serious now. "Fair. But she didn't shut you down."

"No. She said I wasn't overstepping. That next time I'd need a better excuse than a thank-you dinner."

"Next time?" Mark echoed. "So, there is a next time."

"Maybe."

Mark leaned back in his chair, then tapped the rim of his coffee mug. "Listen, Ethan, I don't want to be a downer..."

"Oh boy," I said. "Here it comes."

"But I saw Sinclair a few weeks ago. At that faculty charity thing."

"Okay?"

"She was with someone."

I frowned. "Another professor?"

"Yeah, tenured at that. Benjamin Harper. He teaches economics. Tall, sharp dresser, always smells like expensive cologne and misplaced superiority."

"Sounds like a joy," I muttered.

"They weren't, like, making out in the lecture hall," Mark added. "But they looked close. Like, inside-jokes-and-eye-contact close."

James tilted his head. "Are you saying they're together?"

Mark raised both hands. "I don't know. Could be nothing. But it didn't look like nothing."

I stared down at my mug, the steam now lazily curling into the space between my furrowed eyebrows.

Benjamin Harper.

I'd heard his name around campus.

Students either loved or hated him. No middle ground. He had a reputation for being brilliant, charismatic, a bit of a pompous ass. The opposite of me in nearly every category.

"Why didn't you say something before?" I asked, not accusing, just confused.

"I didn't know you were actively auditioning to be her romantic subplot," Mark replied, shrugging. "And honestly, I thought it was one of those faculty-faculty flings. Nothing serious."

James leaned forward. "Does this change how you feel?"

I swallowed. That was the question, wasn't it?

"I don't know," I said finally. "I mean yeah, maybe. If she's seeing someone, that's obviously important. But she didn't say anything last night. She didn't act like she was taken."

James raised an eyebrow. "Would she tell you?"

Another excellent question.

Olivia was private. Composed.

She wore boundaries like tailored clothes just tight enough to remind you not to get too close. If she were seeing someone, she'd keep it concealed, especially with a student.

Especially with me.

Mark tapped his fork against his plate. "If you're gonna get your heart broken, you should at least know the terrain first."

"You sound like a romantic and a therapist," I said.

"Just looking out for you," he replied, surprisingly sincere.

James clapped a hand on my shoulder. "Okay, let's think this through logically. Did she give you any signals that there was someone else?"

I replayed the night in my mind.

Every smile, every laugh, every moment, her eyes lingered on mine for just a second too long.

"No," I said. "Nothing that suggested she was attached. But also, nothing that said she wasn't."

"So," Mark said, "we're officially in Ambiguity City."

"Population: me."

James snorted. "So, what's the move now?"

I rubbed a hand over my face. "I don't know. I guess. I wait. Be normal. Finish the semester. Don't turn into a lovesick idiot."

Mark gave me a look. "Too late."

I threw a pillow at him.

They laughed, but the thought stuck in my mind like a splinter: What if there was someone else? What if I'd just walked straight into a situation where I was always going to be the subplot and never the ending?

I sipped my coffee again, letting the bitterness steady me. No matter what, I knew one thing for sure: I didn't regret last night.

Not a second of it.

And maybe the next six weeks would reveal what kind of story this really was.

Whether I was just a charming interruption...

Or something more.

9

The Wingman

It was loud. Like always.

Glasses clinking, bass thudding overhead, and the hum of Friday night madness growing with every person who stumbled through the door. I was in the thick of it behind the bar, sleeves rolled to my elbows, towel slung over my shoulder, doing what I did best, pouring drinks and pretending I had it all together.

Bartending wasn't the dream.

It would never be the thing I did forever.

But it paid my third of the rent, and it kept me from spiralling into my head. Out here, in the chaos and chatter, I felt grounded. In control.

Hell, sometimes I even felt cool.

I'd crack a joke, flip a bottle, flash a grin, and people laughed like I belonged in this world. Like I was somebody.

And then she walked in.

I didn't see her right away.

I didn't feel the air shift, the sudden weight of being watched. I was too busy charming a group of girls who were leaning a little too close over the bar, all flirty eyes, and slurred compliments. That was when she spotted me. Professor Olivia Sinclair. And right beside her, Benjamin Harper.

Yeah. That Benjamin Harper. Just like Mark had described him.

The one I thought might be more than just a friend to her.

She didn't know I worked here.

That much was obvious.

Her eyes locked on me, wide with surprise and then narrowed slightly, like she was trying to recalibrate how she saw me. I wasn't the guy fumbling through theories in her lecture hall right now. I was someone else.

Confident.

In control.

I caught the flicker of something in her face.

Interest? Confusion?

I couldn't tell. But it made my chest tighten.

They took a booth in the corner, away from the noise.

Classy. Low profile.

But I still caught her glancing my way. Just once. And it threw me.

Ten minutes later, I looked up and boom. There she was again, just staring straight at me.

She looked, damn it, beautiful.

Black blouse, sleeves rolled just enough to be dangerous, silver earrings catching the light. She didn't belong in a bar like this, half-sticky floors, too-loud laughter, and cheap beer smells, but somehow, she made it look like the bar was the thing that didn't belong.

And the crazy part? She was still watching me.

I pretended to be focused on the drink in front of me, but my heart kicked up a gear. My hands stayed steady, thank God, but I could feel her eyes following me, even when I wasn't facing her.

It hit me then; Olivia Sinclair was watching me in my element.

And weirdly, I liked it.

Out here, I wasn't the awkward guy who dropped his fork into the risotto. I wasn't the kid with too many questions and a secret crush on his professor. Out here, I was the bartender. I was someone.

I spotted Benjamin watching her, though.

The way he looked at her. Quiet, thoughtful, almost like he was studying the sky before it rains. There was something deep there, but not romantic. No. It felt older than that. Worn-in, like two people who'd seen each other through a lot of storms.

So, when Benjamin stood and told her he was grabbing drinks, she barely nodded, still half-watching me.

I didn't think anything of it until he stepped up to the bar and waved me over.

"Hey there," he said, all an effortless charm.

"What can I get you?" I asked, already reaching for a glass.

"Two bourbons neat. One with a splash of water."

I nodded and started pouring.

"You're good at this," he said, watching my hands. "Fast. Confident. I bet the tips are solid."

"Not bad on Fridays," I replied, keeping my tone light.

"You look like someone who knows how to work a room," he said.

I gave a small shrug. "Something like that."

Then he hit me with it. "You ever date students from your university?"

I blinked. Hard. "No. Definitely not. That'd be yeah, no. Bad idea."

He smiled like he already knew the answer. "Smart move. But you're not just a student, are you? You've got more poise than most I've seen."

Then it clicked. Damn, I am slow. My stomach dropped. "Wait. You're faculty?"

"Economics," he said, offering his hand. "Benjamin Harper."

Boom. There it was. The name I'd been low-key obsessing over since Mark dropped it.

I shook his hand, trying not to look as rattled as I felt. The guy Olivia might be seeing, and he was standing here, smiling at me, reading me like a damn book.

"You know a lot about people," I said cautiously.

"Comes with age," he said with a little shrug. "You know what I see when I look at you?"

I braced myself. "What?"

"A guy who's into someone he thinks he shouldn't be into. And someone who's being watched like he's the only person in the room."

My throat dried out. "That obvious?"

He smiled gently. "Only to someone who knows her."

I stared, heart hammering.

"She deserves to be seen like that," he added.

And then I had to ask.

"You're not... with her?"

He let out a deep laugh. "God, no. Olivia's basically my sister. She made me sit through three Nicholas Sparks movies when my Robert died. That kind of trauma bonds people."

I blinked. "So, you're not..."

"Nope. Just her fake plus-one, her wingman, when she wants to avoid questions at faculty events. But if you're thinking about asking her questions," he leaned, "do it before someone else does."

"What questions?" I asked.

"Micah Hale. Her fiancé. Lost in Afghanistan in 2013. And my partner, Robert. Both gone over twelve years now. We carried each other through it. You did not know?"

I just stared at him.

He gave me a wink. "Good luck, bartender."

Then he walked away like he hadn't just cracked open my chest and exposed my heart.

Back at their booth, Olivia raised a brow as he sat down.

"What took so long?"

Benjamin sipped his bourbon. "Your bartender's got charm. I was taking notes."

She smiled a little, but her eyes went back to me.

"You know him?" he asked, not even trying to hide the grin.

She paused. "He's one of my students."

Benjamin blinked. "Well, hell. Now it makes sense. He is your TA. Right?"

She gave him a look. "Yes. You didn't?"

"Nope. I just thought he was a well-spoken college kid with great arms."

She sighed. But her lips twitched.

"You're impossible."

"True. But also, not blind." He raised his glass toward me. "He's got heart. And you? You looked like someone who forgot how to blink."

She didn't answer. Just looked at me again.

And that look said everything I'd been hoping for.

10

It Started Here

By the time the clock hit 2:00 a.m., my feet were numb, my shoulders ached, and my voice had dropped half an octave from shouting over bass and beer orders. The crowd had thinned to the usual late-night stragglers and heartbreak drinkers, and I was just about ready to melt into the floor.

I gave my final nod to Leo, the other bartender on shift, tossed my towel into the bin, and headed to the back to grab my hoodie. The second I stepped out from behind the bar and into the space where patrons were still finishing their drinks, the air felt, well, different.

Like someone was waiting for me.

I tried not to look. I tried. But some magnetic pull dragged my eyes to the corner booth.

She was still there.

Olivia.

Her black blouse had creased ever so slightly from how long she'd been sitting. Her arms were crossed loosely, her body turned in toward Benjamin—but her eyes were on me.

Again.

Benjamin caught my glance and gave me the faintest nod. Just a small one.

Like, your move, kid.

I took a breath and walked past them, toward the door, heart pounding like I'd just done a double shot of espresso. I didn't expect anything. Maybe a wave, a polite nod. Maybe nothing at all.

But then...

"Ethan."

Her voice. Clear. Even over the dying hum of music.

I turned, slowly.

She stood now, away from the booth, hands clasped in front of her like she wasn't sure what to do with them. Olivia always carried herself with composure, but right now, I saw something else in her expression: uncertainty.

Curiosity?

Maybe even nerves.

"I didn't know you worked here," she said, tucking a strand of hair behind her ear.

I chuckled softly, rubbing the back of my neck. "Yeah. Guess it's a little different from the classroom version of me."

Her lips curved. "You're good at it."

"Thanks," I said. "It's mostly smoke and mirrors."

"No," she said, shaking her head just slightly. "You're different out here. Confident. At ease."

I shrugged, trying not to let that land too hard. "It's easier when no one's grading me."

She smiled, just a touch, and stepped closer. Not enough to draw attention, but enough that I could feel the space between us shrink. She smelled like something soft and floral layered over old books and something stronger I couldn't name.

"You and Professor Harper," I said, careful. "You're close."

Her brows lifted, but not in surprise. "We've been friends a long time."

"He's not..."

"Mine?" she offered.

I nodded, pulse thrumming in my ears.

"No," she said softly. "Not like that. We both suffered in the past, and those events brought us and kept us together."

I exhaled, slow.

She tilted her head. "He said you were charming. I didn't believe him."

"Oh?" I said, grinning despite myself. "And what do you believe now?"

Her gaze lingered. "I think you're hard to look away from when you're being yourself."

I didn't know what to say to that. I felt heat rise in my chest, spreading under my skin like wildfire. I looked away, just for a second. When I looked back, her expression had softened.

"I know this is complicated," she said quietly. "I'm not blind to it."

"No," I said. "Neither am I."

A beat of silence stretched between us, filled only with the sound of chairs scraping and the faint thump of closing-time playlists. Her eyes searched mine like she was trying to read a language she didn't quite understand.

"Do you want to walk a bit?" she asked suddenly. "Clear your head. Or mine."

I blinked. "Yeah. I'd like that."

Benjamin stood then, nodding to both of us as he pulled on his coat. "I'll catch you tomorrow," he said to her, giving me one last amused smile before disappearing out the door.

I held it open for her as we stepped outside.

The night was cool, the air kissed with rain that hadn't quite arrived yet. The streets were mostly empty now, just the occasional cab gliding by, headlights casting flickers of gold on the sidewalk.

We walked in silence for a while. Not awkward, though. Not heavy. Just thoughtful.

Finally, Olivia spoke.

"After Micah died," she said slowly, "I didn't think I'd ever feel anything again. Not like that. Not even close. Not this real."

I said nothing. I didn't interrupt. Just listened.

"And I'm not saying I do. I'm not saying this is something," she added, glancing over at me. "But I haven't looked at someone like that in a long time."

My breath caught. "Like what?"

"Like the way I looked at you tonight," she said. "Like someone who made the room a little quieter just by being in it."

I stopped walking.

She did too, turning to face me. The streetlight behind her haloed her hair in soft gold. Her eyes were shadowed and sharp all at once.

"I don't know what this is," I said, voice low. "But I know what it isn't."

"What?"

"It isn't one-sided."

She looked at me for a long moment.

Then she smiled a small smile, but real.

"I should go," she said, though she didn't move.

I nodded. "Okay."

Neither of us turned away.

"Goodnight, Ethan."

"Goodnight, Olivia."

She walked a few steps before turning back once, just briefly.

And for the first time since I walked into her class, I felt like we were standing on equal ground.

Maybe the story hadn't started in the classroom.

I realised maybe it started here.

And it wasn't a mistake.

11

Real Feeling

Each step echoed louder than it should have on the quiet street, like the city was trying to force me to hear myself think.

Too late for that.

The night air was crisp against my skin, but I barely felt it. I was still holding on to the warmth of his presence, the way he looked at me under that streetlight, like I was the only thing that mattered in a world full of noise. It had been a long time since someone looked at me that way. A long time since I'd allowed myself to see someone back.

God, what was I doing?

He was my student.

My student.

But that truth felt smaller than it should've tonight. Not insignificant, but not the full picture, either. Because the truth was, Ethan had never felt like just a student to me.

I knew it the first time he stayed after class to ask for help concerning my lecture. He asked with the kind of curiosity I rarely saw anymore. Most students ask to impress. He asked because he wanted to understand. And when he listened, really listened, it felt like I was being heard for the first time in years and how easily we changed directions into a quick discussion of science fiction and fantasy authors.

I shouldn't have gone to that bar tonight.

Benjamin had suggested it on a whim. "Let's get out," he said. "You're turning into a hermit with a coffee addiction."

I hadn't expected to see Ethan there.

And I definitely hadn't expected to see him like that.

Behind the bar, he was magnetic. He was effortless. His laugh came easy, his smile even easier. Girls leaned into him like gravity was his to command. The girls loved him. And he didn't even seem to notice. He was in his skin in a way I rarely saw him at school—confident, unafraid, free.

I'd been staring. I knew it. And Benjamin, ever the hawk, had noticed, of course.

When he got up to get us drinks, I knew exactly what he was doing. He was trying to read Ethan. Benjamin always had a nose for people. And apparently, matchmaking. I hadn't told him who Ethan was. Not until he returned with a knowing smile and a pointed eyebrow raised in silent accusation.

"He's one of my students," I'd said, like I was confessing to a crime.

Benjamin had just laughed. "He's also not a child."

The walk back to my apartment felt longer than usual. Every corner of the city was still wide awake, but my mind had tunnelled in. On him. On me. On this strange, impossible pull between us.

I should've ended it right there. Told him we couldn't do this. Reminded him, and myself, that lines existed for a reason.

But I didn't.

Because when I looked into Ethan's eyes tonight, I didn't see a student. I saw a man. A kind and thoughtful, gentle man. One who saw the cracks in me and didn't flinch.

And I was tired of pretending like I felt nothing.

When I finally got home, I locked the door behind me, kicked off my heels, and stood in the middle of my kitchen, unsure of what to do with my hands.

My phone buzzed. It was Benjamin.

You good?

I stared at the message for a second. Then replied.

I don't know.

He didn't type back right away. But when he did, it was just three words.

Let yourself feel.

Damn him.

I set the phone down and walked to the window, arms folded across my chest, heart hammering like I'd just walked out of a first date that meant too much.

Maybe this was all a bad idea.

Maybe I'd get burned.

But maybe not.

Maybe something good had slipped into my life when I wasn't looking. Maybe I didn't have to keep pretending I was fine walking through life alone. Micah was gone. That ache would never leave. But that didn't mean I had to close myself off forever.

I thought of Ethan's voice, the way he said, "It isn't one-sided."

It wasn't. Not even close.

A soft, unexpected smile pulled at my lips.

Tomorrow, we'd both wake up, and the rules would return. The classroom. The expectations. The thousand things left unsaid.

But tonight? Tonight, I was letting myself feel.

And for the first time in years, that didn't terrify me.

12

Hide and Seek

James, Mark, and I did not want to be at this event.

Mandatory faculty-student mixer.

Wine in plastic cups. Cheddar cubes pretending to be fancy cheese.

Jazz playlist from Spotify.

Still, we showed up. Because not showing up would've raised more eyebrows than attending with a forced smile and a name tag that read "Hi, I'm Ethan," even though every professor here still called me Mr. Carter like I was presenting a thesis instead of nursing a beer.

Benjamin was already working the room like a seasoned politician.

Charming, laughing too loud, playfully stealing cookies off students' plates. I caught his eye across the room, and he winked.

I hadn't seen Olivia yet. I told myself I wasn't looking for her.

But I was.

The last time I saw her; she'd looked at me like she might actually feel what I was feeling. Then she walked away before I could say anything more.

It had been a week of long lectures and longer silences. She didn't avoid me.

But she didn't exactly seek me out either.

Which, I guess, made sense.

I was still telling myself all of this was a harmless crush. Something I'd tuck away and laugh about years from now when I was older and less idiotic.

And then Olivia walked in.

Black blazer. Dark jeans. Hair up, a few loose strands curling near her temple. She was scanning the room, smile practiced, calm, until her eyes landed on me, and I saw it.

That flicker.

Not surprise.

Recognition.

Like I was something she had spent the week trying not to remember.

I looked away first.

That was when Benjamin, clearly bored, clapped his hands together like a misbehaving camp counsellor. "Alright!" he called out. "We've got ten minutes before this becomes completely unbearable. Who's up for something ridiculous?"

Groans.

A few curious laughs. Someone whispered, "Please no icebreakers."

Benjamin grinned. "Relax. No name games. Simply good old-fashioned hide-and-seek."

The room blinked at him.

"This is ridiculous Benjamin. You cannot mean it."

"No way I am doing this," shouted someone from the back of the room.

"How much more wine do we have left?" someone said, and everyone laughed aloud.

"You're joking," Olivia said, crossing her arms, amused and exasperated at once.

He grinned wider. "Students and faculty hide. I will be the first seeker. No complaints. You've all had wine. You're relaxed. This'll be the most fun you've had since tenure was invented."

I expected her to roll her eyes and shut it down. Instead, to my total shock, she sighed and said, "Fine. But don't expect me to crawl under anything dusty looking for a student," which brought laughter from many faculty members and students.

Fifteen minutes later, I was crouching behind a stack of broken bar stools in the staff closet room and wondering what decisions in my life led me to hiding from a professor like a criminal, avoiding tax season.

Then the door opened.

And she slipped in.

Olivia.

She didn't see me at first. She was too busy scanning the dark corners of the room. The lights were off. All I could see was her silhouette in the glow from the hallway, the way she closed the door quickly behind her like she was running from someone.

We both saw the same thing at once: the open coat closet.

She whispered, "Move."

I scrambled in first. She followed, closing the door behind us, and suddenly the world shrank to four claustrophobic feet and the warm scent of her perfume.

We didn't speak at first. Just stood in the dark. Too close.

Our arms brushed.

I held my breath.

"This is ridiculous," she muttered softly. I could feel her voice, not just hear it. "We are adults."

"I know," I whispered.

A beat passed. Silence.

Then she said: "Benjamin is the devil."

That made me laugh. Not loud. Just a soft exhale that stirred the air between us.

She didn't move away.

Neither did I.

"You've been quiet," I said finally.

She hesitated. "So have you."

"I didn't want to make things harder."

"Too late."

That stopped me.

I turned a little, just enough that I could see the faintest glint of her profile. Her lips. Her lashes. She was staring straight ahead, like if she looked at me, this whole thing would combust.

"Ethan," she said, voice low and trembling slightly. "We can't do this."

"I know," I said. "But I want to."

She said nothing.

My heart was pounding in my throat now, loud enough I was sure she could hear it.

She turned then. Slightly. Just her face. And we were inches apart in the dark. One deep breath from crossing a line.

And then it happened. I didn't mean to kiss her.

Honestly.

It wasn't planned. It wasn't some calculated move. I think maybe I was trying to speak again. Or maybe she was. Either way, our lips brushed. A soft, accidental collision, like the world leaned just a little too far.

And neither of us pulled away.

Her breath caught. My hands lifted instinctively, one brushing her waist, the other steadying myself against the wall. She didn't stop me. Her fingers curled into the front of my shirt like she needed something to hold on to. And then her lips were pressing into mine, deeper now, deliberate.

Real.

The closet was still. My head was spinning.

It was the kind of kiss you feel in your spine. The kind you remember.

And then, just as suddenly, she pulled back.

Breathing hard. Eyes wide.

We stood there; the silence was so thick it could've been screaming.

"We can't," she said again, softer now. Less conviction this time. More ache.

"I know," I whispered.

But neither of us moved.

Again, I held her in my arms and kissed her. This time with a sensitive passion to let her know I wanted her, and I could tell she felt the same.

"We can't," she said again, but I was not convinced.

Outside, the sound of footsteps and laughter filled the hallway.

Inside that tiny coat closet, everything had changed.

13

Olivia

I didn't sleep that night.

Every time I closed my eyes, I felt the press of his mouth again, tentative at first, and then terrifyingly certain. I kept thinking I should've stopped it sooner. That if I'd had an ounce more self-control, I wouldn't have leaned in. I wouldn't have grabbed the front of his shirt like I needed it to stay grounded. Like I needed him.

But the truth was, I had wanted to. God, I had wanted to.

And that scared me more than I could admit.

The next morning, I was at my desk by six, staring blankly at my laptop, re-reading the same paragraph in a grant proposal I'd written months ago, pretending like my life hadn't been turned inside out by a kiss in a coat closet.

A kiss.

With a student.

A student who made me laugh without trying, who paid attention in ways that made me feel seen, not as a professor, but as a person. Who had no idea how close I was to losing the balance I'd spent years rebuilding.

I told myself it didn't mean anything. That it was just the darkness and the proximity and Benjamin's ridiculous game.

I told myself a lot of things I didn't believe.

I avoided the department lounge all day. I ducked out of two meetings. I ignored Benjamin's texts.

And then, in the early evening, he showed up at my office.

Ethan.

I heard the knock and froze. Somehow, I already knew it was him.

I took a breath. "Come in."

He stepped in slowly, like he wasn't sure he had the right to. His eyes met mine, and it was all there. The tension. The confusion. The memory.

He closed the door behind him.

"I'm sorry," he said, before I could say anything.

I opened my mouth, then closed it again. My throat was dry.

"You did nothing wrong? You didn't force me? You didn't mean it?"

All of it felt false.

He stepped forward. "Oh, I meant it. I didn't mean to cross a line, but I did."

"You didn't," I said too quickly.

He blinked. "I kissed you."

"I kissed you back."

There was a pause, the kind that holds its breath.

I looked away. "It can't be something."

He nodded slowly, like he'd already had that conversation with himself. "I know. You're faculty. I'm a student. You're—"

"—my student," I said, cutting him off. "There are rules."

"But I'm not in your class anymore. Early this morning, I dropped the course."

"That doesn't matter, Ethan."

He ran a hand through his hair. "So, what do we do? Pretend it didn't happen?"

My chest tightened. "We have to."

He looked like I'd slapped him. Just a flicker of pain across his face before he masked it with a tight nod.

"Okay," he said. "If that's what you want."

I didn't answer.

Because I wasn't sure what I wanted.

He turned, then hesitated. "I'm not trying to make your life harder, Olivia. I swear. I've just never felt like this about anyone before. And I'm not some dumb kid. I know what this could cost you. I know the risks."

My heart cracked open a little more. "Then you understand why this has to stop."

He nodded again. "I do."

He left without another word.

And I sat there in the silence, wishing I could go back to a time before a kiss rewrote everything I thought I knew about myself.

A few days passed. We didn't speak. We didn't text. We avoided eye contact in the halls.

Benjamin, of course, noticed everything.

"You two are being weird," he said one afternoon, balancing a coffee on a stack of folders.

"I don't know what you're talking about," I replied, typing furiously into a document I wasn't actually reading.

"Oh, please," he said, sitting across from me uninvited. "You've been sulking for days, and Ethan looks like someone kicked his puppy."

I shot him a look. "You don't know anything."

He gave me a pointed stare. "You kissed him, didn't you?"

I said nothing.

He smiled. "Olivia. You did."

I covered my face with my hands. "It was a mistake. You set us up."

"I nudged fate."

"You trapped us in a closet."

"A spacious closet," he said, grinning.

I sighed and leaned back. "It doesn't matter. Nothing's going to happen."

He raised an eyebrow. "Are you saying that because it's the right thing, or because you're afraid?"

I stared at the ceiling. "Both."

Benjamin grew quiet for a moment. Then he said softly, "Olivia, I've seen you survive hell and back. Don't convince yourself you don't deserve something real because you're scared of losing control."

I closed my eyes.

But I didn't answer.

Because the part of me that wanted Ethan, the real, honest, messy part, was growing louder by the day.

And I didn't know how much longer I could keep ignoring it.

14

Ethan

I didn't see Olivia for a week after that conversation in her office.

Didn't seek her out. Didn't hover in doorways or loiter near the faculty lounge hoping to catch her eye.

I meant what I said.

I wasn't here to make her life harder.

But that didn't mean I was giving up.

Not even close.

Something had shifted in me after that kiss—and not just because of how it happened, or who it was with. It was like the world had suddenly tilted on a new axis, and I wasn't interested in going back to how things were before. Not just with her—but with me.

So, I made some changes.

I dropped a couple of electives that weren't serving me and took on an accelerated course plan with a focus on something that had always quietly tugged at my curiosity: social impact entrepreneurship. Business with a purpose. Building something that helped people, not just profits.

It wasn't a flashy pivot, but it felt right. And the new advisor told me if I played it right and took two summer intensives, I could graduate earlier than expected.

Maybe even by the end of next year.

I started spending my extra hours at a shared workspace downtown, surrounded by people who were dreaming loud and building fast. I took my laptop, my notebooks, and occasionally a cold brew that could strip paint off the walls, and dove into case studies, design thinking, impact models. It was chaos. It was thrilling.

It was also a distraction.

Because when I wasn't reading, or planning, or answering group chats about a hypothetical eco-startup, I was thinking about her.

About Olivia.

The way her voice dropped when she was trying not to laugh. The way she said my name when she was angry—or worse, trying not to be. That night in the closet, the soft shock in her breath just before we kissed. The part of her that said no with her words and wait with her eyes.

But I didn't reach out.

I figured... if I mattered at all, she'd come to me when she was ready.

And if she didn't—well.

At least I'd be someone worth finding when she looked again.

It was a Tuesday when I saw her next.

I was in line at the café near campus, earbuds in, answering emails on my phone when I glanced up—and there she was. Black wool coat, scarf wrapped once around her neck, hair half pulled back like she'd gotten distracted mid-style.

She looked tired.

Beautiful, but tired.

She didn't see me at first. She was focused on the pastries behind the glass. I thought about ducking out, pretending I hadn't noticed. Giving her more space.

But before I could turn, she looked up.

And saw me.

Her eyes widened, and something flickered in them— uncertainty, maybe. Hesitation. And then... warmth.

She stepped forward.

I pulled out my earbuds. "Hey."

"Hi," she said, voice soft. "You've been... quiet."

I nodded. "Trying not to cause any more trouble."

She looked down, then back at me. "You're no trouble, Ethan."

That surprised me more than it should've.

Before I could say anything, the barista called my name. I stepped up, grabbed my drink, and turned back to her.

"You want to sit?" I asked. "No pressure. Just coffee."

She hesitated, then gave the smallest nod. "Okay."

We found a table by the window. I took the seat across from her and tried not to watch her too closely as she stirred her drink.

"You changed your schedule," she said after a moment.

I blinked. "How'd you know?"

She shrugged lightly. "I saw your name come off the independent study list. And Benjamin mentioned something about you shifting majors."

"Yeah," I said, a little sheepish. "I needed a reset. Something with more purpose."

She studied me. "That's good. That's fantastic."

I gave a small smile. "Feels good."

A pause.

Then she said, "I've been thinking about what you said. About the kiss. About everything."

My stomach tightened.

"I don't want to be the reason you hold back," she continued. "Or the reason you get stuck in a complicated grey zone."

"You're not," I said immediately. "You're the reason I'm moving forward. I don't know how else to explain it. You challenged me, Olivia. You still do."

Her eyes dropped to the lid of her coffee cup.

"I've been alone for a long time," she said, barely above a whisper. "Not in the literal sense, but in the way that matters. Since Micah. Since the war took him. And I thought... that was just how it was going to be. That I didn't get to have something light again. Or fun. Or messy. Or hopeful."

My chest ached.

"I don't want to hurt you," she added. "I don't want to cross a line that ruins what we've both worked hard for."

"I don't want perfect," I said. "I want real. And I can wait. However long it takes. I'm not going anywhere."

She looked up at me, her eyes glassy, and for a second, I could swear I saw the wall inside her shift.

Crack.

Not collapse.

But shift.

She smiled, just a little. "You're stubborn."

"Borderline relentless."

She chuckled, and it was the first genuine sound of hope I'd heard from her in days.

"Listen, I am going to a literary conference, and I will be gone for a couple of days. I just wanted you to know."

I smiled. "Well, my new course has me going to a conference of my own, which takes me away as well for a few days. How about we catch up later?"

"Yes, I'd love to do that. Compare notes, sort of speak," Olivia said.

"Yeah," I said.

And that was enough for now.

15

Processing Error

It was supposed to be a quiet weekend.

A literary conference. Three days. Two panels. One keynote, Professor Grant Bathurst, where I was actually excited to attend his symposium. And most importantly, no Ethan.

I hadn't seen him in over a week since our coffee and conversation. And I'd convinced myself that a little physical distance would help me sort out the whirlwind he'd left in my chest.

Spoiler: It hadn't.

Still, I was proud of myself for booking the weekend away. A cozy little hotel outside the city, far from campus, and even farther from all the complications of my professional life. It was time to focus on me, the kind of me who wore tailored blazers and asked pretentious questions during Q&As. The kind of me who absolutely did not have feelings for a student.

And then Ethan freaking Carter walked out of the lift.

Dragging a duffel bag.

Wearing a conference badge.

In my hotel.

I blinked so hard I momentarily wondered if I'd had one too many of those free lobby mimosas.

"Ethan?"

His head snapped toward me, and the look on his face was one of pure, unfiltered panic.

"Olivia?" he said, his voice going high-pitched in a way that would've been funny if I wasn't too busy clutching my tote bag like it could protect me from reality. "What? Wait. You're here?"

I folded my arms. "Yes, I am here. At my literary conference. Which, judging by your expression, is not where you expected me to be."

He glanced down at his badge and scratched the back of his neck. "Yeah, uh... tech and innovation summit. They moved venues last minute. I didn't realise it was... shared."

Of course they did. Of course, the hotel was double-booked. Of course, the universe had a terrible sense of humour and a subscription to ironic timing.

We stared at each other for a beat too long.

Then, in unison, we said, "You're not supposed to be here."

And somehow that made us both laugh.

Things escalated quickly after that.

First, the front desk informed Ethan that because of a "processing error" and "unexpectedly high attendance," the hotel had double-booked his room.

"And the only available room left," the concierge chirped sweetly, "is the one already reserved under the name Olivia Sinclair."

"Nope," I said, before the concierge could even finish. "No. Absolutely not. I'm not sharing a room with him."

But Ethan was already laughing, shaking his head. "It's okay. I'll sleep in the conference hall. Or the lobby. Or the pool, if they'll let me."

"Sir," the concierge said, sounding vaguely terrified, "you legally can't sleep in the pool."

Eventually, we settled it like civilised adults: two queen beds, zero funny business or so we hoped, and a stack of complimentary drink vouchers to soothe my rapidly fraying nerves.

By evening, things had started to feel almost normal.

We were walking back from our respective panels he energised from a workshop on sustainable writing; me mildly traumatised from a roundtable on poetry in the postmodern age when we passed the hotel lounge and heard it.

The unmistakable sound of someone butchering "Total Eclipse of the Heart" on karaoke.

We froze.

Then looked at each other.

Then, in perfect sync, said, "No way."

Five minutes later, I was clutching a microphone, Ethan was dramatically pointing at invisible stars, and we were doing the most tragic, theatrical duet of Bonnie Tyler's career. People clapped. Someone threw a napkin rose. I think a man in the corner wept.

When we finally collapsed into our booth, breathless and slightly wine-drunk, Ethan leaned back and said, "That was the worst thing I've ever done."

"You say that," I said, "but your falsetto was disturbingly accurate."

He grinned.

And for a moment, it wasn't complicated.

We weren't student and professor. Weren't grief and guilt and maybes tangled in rules.

We were just two idiots at a karaoke bar in a hotel that didn't understand personal boundaries.

Back in the room, I changed in the bathroom while he respectfully faced the wall and argued with the hotel's streaming service over whether The Mummy was "free with ads" or "a cruel lie."

When I came out in sweatpants and a hoodie, he glanced up and gave me a smile so soft it made my chest ache.

"What?" I said.

"Nothing," he said, already flipping onto his bed. "It's you just look like someone who might be convinced to sing Journey next."

I tossed a pillow at him. "Don't tempt me."

But in truth?

I wanted to.

I wanted to be tempted.

And that terrified me more than anything.

16

Jealousy is Just a Really Awkward Feeling

If jealousy had a flavour, it would taste like bitter hotel coffee and the sound of Olivia laughing at some guy's joke two tables over.

I was halfway through my dry toast, trying to focus on my keynote prep and not spiral into something out of a teenage diary, when I saw him.

Professor Grant Bathurst.

Tan. Crisp. Perfect hair. The kind of man who probably volunteers to do his taxes early. And there he was, leaning against the breakfast buffet like he owned the concept of granola, making Olivia laugh.

Laugh and laugh and laugh, ad nauseam.

The throw-your-head-back, touch-the-other-person's-arm kind of laugh.

I chewed my toast harder.

Mark had warned me about this. "You give someone space, and someone else just waltzes into it with better shoes."

Grant's shoes were beautiful. Italian. I hated them immediately.

Olivia didn't even notice me slinking toward the coffee dispenser like a caffeinated phantom of the opera. I told myself I wasn't eavesdropping; I was just hydrating and observing in a totally chill and reasonable way.

That was until I heard him say,

"You know, if you're free tonight, there's this reading I'm doing at the Rose Room. You'd look incredible against velvet lighting."

Velvet lighting?

VELVET LIGHTING.

Who even talks like that outside of poetry slams and cologne commercials?

I nearly choked on my coffee. I had to act.

I couldn't just stand there like a side character while Smooth-Professor-Grant-With-the-Greco-Roman-Jawline Bathurst tried to whisk Olivia off into his pretentious-lit-mag sunset.

No.

If this was going to be dumb and dramatic, then I was going to be dumber and more dramatic.

That afternoon, I showed up at Olivia's panel dressed to kill in my conference blazer, all black turtleneck, and tragic soul.

I sat in the front row.

I nodded pensively.

I even took furious notes that I would never read, just so she'd notice me scribbling her brilliance like I was going to translate it into sonnets later.

When she opened the floor to questions, I stood and asked, "How does the existential weight of longing impact the narrative voice when the desire feels... forbidden?"

She blinked. Someone in the back whispered, "Whoa."

Olivia arched a brow and said slowly, "I think that might be more of a personal question."

"It is," I said. "It's very personal."

There were actual gasps.

I may have accidentally turned her panel into a soap opera.

Grant was in the second row, smirking like a man who thought he'd already won.

Challenge accepted Professor Grant.

Later that evening, the hotel lounge was hopping again, and naturally, Olivia showed up in a deep green dress that made me question if anything in life had ever been fair.

Grant was with her, of course. He held out her chair. Ordered her a cocktail with confidence. Probably knew the bartender by name.

I waited.

Watched.

And then, when the karaoke sign-up list came around, I made my move.

They were mid-conversation when the opening notes of "I Will Always Love You" started echoing through the room.

People turned. I took the stage.

Olivia froze.

Grant's drink paused halfway to his lips.

I gripped the mic like a man ready to walk into battle and softly, painfully, warbled my way through the most unhinged Whitney Houston rendition ever heard by mortal ears.

It was tragic.

It was brave.

It was theatrical.

I pointed at Olivia during the key change. Someone near the bar screamed, "He's in love!"

By the time I hit the final high note, which was really more of a yodel, I dropped to one knee like I'd just been stabbed by Cupid's most dramatic arrow.

Silence.

Then wild applause.

Grant looked like he'd just swallowed a bug.

Olivia stared at me. Somewhere between horrified and impressed?

She found me later, outside by the garden terrace, where I was nursing my pride and a surprisingly good gin and tonic.

"So," she said, leaning on the railing beside me, "going for subtlety, were we?"

I didn't look at her. "Subtleties for cowards."

She laughed. Actually laughed.

"I wasn't going to go with him, you know," she said after a minute. "To the Rose Room."

I looked at her then. "No?"

She shook her head. "He's got great teeth. But I hate velvet lighting."

We both smiled.

Then she nudged me. "You're ridiculous."

"Yeah, but you watched the whole song."

"I did," she said, eyes soft.

I took a breath. "So, what now?"

She didn't answer right away. Just reached for my hand, laced her fingers through mine like it was something she'd done a hundred times before.

And for a second, the world didn't feel quite so messy.

17

Alarm Bells

Back on campus, the air felt different.

Maybe it was the way people looked at me now, more curious, less casual. Or maybe it was me, paranoid and hyperaware after the chaos of the hotel weekend. Either way, there was no denying that the walls of fiction and reality were beginning to thin.

And the whispers were starting.

I'd barely made it two steps into the quad before I ran into Professor Bellamy from sociology. She gave me a tight smile, the kind that carried just enough curiosity to suggest she'd heard something. Maybe not everything, but enough. She adjusted her glasses and asked me how my conference went. I told her it was "illuminating," which was apparently not the answer she expected because she nodded slowly, said "Mm-hmm," and then floated away like a curious hawk who smelled fresh scandal.

Then there was my seminar in Modern Ethics, where a question about power dynamics in personal relationships triggered a fit of coughing. I was sure it was covering laughter. James texted me mid-lecture: "Bet that question hit like a freight train. You good, Romeo?"

So, yeah. Subtlety? Not our strong suit.

I did my best to pull back. Give Olivia space. Let her breathe.

After the kiss, after Grant, after everything, I knew she needed time to figure out what this was, or if it even should be anything. And as much as it killed me to wait, to wonder, I respected her enough to not push. I focused on my classes. I dove into the new track I'd picked up, an interdisciplinary program that would actually fast-track my graduation. If I kept pace, I could be out by spring. Which meant this forbidden dance of ours might not stay forbidden for much longer.

Still, avoiding her on campus was like trying to avoid gravity.

We orbited the same halls, the same faculty mixers, the same awkwardly labelled "student-faculty dialogues." Each time, our eyes would catch, and a hundred unspoken things would flare in the space between us.

And, of course, the universe being what it is, the faculty board caught wind of everything at the worst possible time.

It started innocently enough: a scheduling oversight.

I was still listed as Olivia's teaching assistant for the upcoming term, even though I'd switched programs. Someone flagged it as "unusual overlap" as they called it. That led to questions.

Questions led to rumours.

Rumours turned into "concerns," and suddenly, Olivia was being called into a meeting with the Dean.

I found out from James, who burst into our dorm like the messenger in a Greek tragedy.

"Dude. Have you seen your professor lately?"

"I've seen a professor," I said, eyeing the two energy drinks he was juggling like he was preparing to reanimate the dead.

"No, like your professor. Sinclair. Word on the vine is the faculty board called her in for a 'professional conduct' chat. You sure things didn't get, I don't know, visible?"

I blinked. "What does that even mean?"

He flopped into my desk chair. "It means maybe next time you make out in a coat closet; you make sure there aren't people hiding in the adjacent broom closet. People talk, man."

I groaned, flopping face-first onto my bed. "We didn't do anything."

"Yeah, well, your face says otherwise every time her name's mentioned."

I pulled a pillow over my head. "I hate everything."

"And yet," James added with unearned cheer, "your love life remains the only thing keeping half the philosophy department entertained. So, you're welcome?"

That afternoon, I sent her a message. Just one line:

"Heard the board's circling. Want me to clear the air?"

She didn't answer until evening.

"Don't. Not yet. Let me handle it."

Classic Olivia.

Cool. Controlled. In charge.

But I wasn't stupid.

I could read between the lines: this wasn't just some minor hiccup. If the board started sniffing around, they could make her life hell.

Career hell.

Reputation hell.

And all because of me.

Or maybe because of us.

That night, I sat in the campus bar staring at the untouched soda in front of me, wondering if love ever came without landmines. Or faculty intervention.

I didn't know what Olivia would do next. Whether she'd fight it or fold. Whether she'd shut me out for good just to survive it.

But I knew one thing.

I wasn't going anywhere.

Not yet.

18

The Meeting

I knew it was coming the moment I saw the subject line in my inbox:

"Faculty Review Inquiry: Scheduled Meeting Confirmation."

The email was short, sterile, and utterly nauseating.

I sat at my desk, blinking at the words like they might rearrange themselves into something less ominous. They didn't.

Meeting with the Faculty Board. Thursday, 3:00 p.m.

Subject: Professional conduct, departmental oversight, and academic boundaries.

The trifecta of doom.

I closed the email and stared out my office window, watching as the light breeze blew the branches of the nearby trees. There was a small willy wagtail committed to what could only be described as an Olympic-level vault from one tree to another. I envied it. So free. So uninvolved with student-professor rumour mills.

Of course, I knew the talk had been circulating.

A look here. A whisper there.

One too many mentions of "unconventional mentorship."

But I'd told myself it was just gossip. That academia thrived on mild scandal and passive-aggressive commentary in faculty meetings.

But this? This was real.

When I walked into the boardroom that Thursday, the unmistakable scent of institutional judgment hit me.

Polished oak.

Weak coffee.

And the subtle air of people who've decided they already know how the story ends.

Dean Wexler sat at the head of the table, flanked by the familiar faces of faculty peers: Chairwoman Price from History, the ever-ambitious Professor Daniels from Political Science, and Associate Provost Heller, who always looked like he'd just eaten a lemon.

"Professor Sinclair," Wexler greeted me with a nod that was neither warm nor hostile. Just clinical.

I returned it with a carefully measured, "Dean."

He gestured to the seat across from him. "Thank you for coming on short notice."

"As requested," I said smoothly, folding my hands in my lap like a very well-behaved scandal.

Daniels leaned forward. "Let's get to it, shall we?"

Ah, subtlety. Not his strength.

Wexler raised a hand. "We're here to clarify a situation that's come to our attention regarding a student under your advisement, a Mr Ethan Carter."

I said nothing.

The name alone rang through the room like a warning bell.

"There have been observations," Price added delicately. "Nothing formally submitted. But enough to raise concern."

"Specifically," Heller cut in, eyes sharp, "there are questions about your relationship with Mr Carter and whether it may breach the university's code of conduct."

I met his gaze evenly. "Ethan was my student. He is no longer in my department, nor is he under my academic supervision."

"A convenient shift of program," Daniels muttered.

I raised a brow. "Are we suggesting students aren't allowed to change their fields of study?"

Wexler cleared his throat before that could snowball. "No one is suggesting misconduct. We're asking for clarity."

Clarity. That word again.

I took a slow breath. "Ethan and I have had a respectful academic relationship. I offered mentorship. He showed promise. He pursued another track, which I supported."

"And yet," Price said softly, "some faculty members have noticed a certain closeness."

I knew what she meant.

The looks.

The unspoken moments.

The karaoke night that somehow ended up in an English department group chat. Thank you, Benjamin.

"It is not against any formal policy for a faculty member and a former student to remain in contact," I said calmly.

Heller tilted his head. "Is that all this is? Contact?"

This was it.

The moment.

The slow unravelling of the thread.

I could lie.

Say yes.

Say I barely knew Ethan.

Let this moment pass like a terrible cold and get on with my perfectly curated career.

But then I remembered the coat closet. The hotel bar. The way he looked at me like I was something he'd never let the world stain.

So, I did something that shocked even me.

I told the truth.

"We're navigating something complicated," I said carefully. "But I assure you, I've done nothing to compromise my role or the university's standards."

The silence that followed was heavy.

Not damning. But definitely not forgiving.

Wexler looked at me with something almost resembling understanding.

"Professor Sinclair," he said at last, "I believe you when you say your intentions were professional. But perception, in our environment, carries as much weight as policy."

I nodded slowly. "I understand."

"There will be a formal note of caution placed on your file," he continued. "No disciplinary action. But we ask that you limit public contact with Mr Carter while on university grounds and avoid situations that could lead to reputational scrutiny. We're not looking to punish. We're looking to protect."

Protect who I wanted to ask. Me? Or them?

But I said nothing.

As I left the room, Daniels leaned over to Heller and muttered something behind his hand. I didn't hear the words, but I didn't need to.

The machine had been set in motion.

Now, it was only a matter of whether we'd survive it.

19

A Clean Story

It started with a stare.

One of those too-long, too-knowing kinds. The kind that doesn't blink. The kind that makes you feel like someone's already written your ending and is just waiting for you to catch up.

Then came the whispers.

They were like background noise at first—easy to brush off. Campus always buzzed with drama, especially when it involved faculty. But then it started sounding more like my name. Paired with hers.

"Did you hear—?"

"He's the one from Sinclair's class..."

"Switched departments right after. That's suspect, right?"

I didn't even realise I was clenching my jaw until Mark elbowed me during lunch and said, "You're gonna grind your teeth into chalk at this rate."

I looked up from my barely touched sandwich. "It's not a big deal."

He raised a brow. "Dude. It's the only thing people are talking about in my English seminar. A female student literally compared you to Mr Darcy with boundary issues."

"Was that a compliment or an insult?"

"Unclear. But I think she meant it horny."

I groaned and shoved the tray away. "This is so messed up. It's not like anything happened while she was my professor."

Mark gave me a look. The kind that's sympathetic but also deeply amused. "Okay. Technically, you're right. But your face every time she walks into a room? Your Shakespearean karaoke? That's what people remember."

"I didn't think anyone recorded that!"

"People didn't need to. Your performance was legendary."

I dropped my head against the table.

"Anyway," he continued, more gently now, "the faculty board already had a meeting with her, didn't they?"

I lifted my head. "Wait? What?"

Mark's face shifted. He hadn't meant to let that slip.

"They what?"

"I thought you knew," he said, wincing. "Word's been going around. Quietly. They called her in for a review or something."

"What kind of review?"

"No idea. But Price and Heller were on the panel. That's like the Avengers of Passive-Aggressive Academia."

I shot up from my seat. "I have to talk to her."

Mark caught my arm. "Ethan. Wait. Don't storm in there with your whole tragic hero thing. This could get worse if you start drawing more attention."

"I am the attention now," I snapped. "Might as well own it."

He sighed. "I swear you were way more chill before you met her."

"Was I?" I muttered, already walking away.

I didn't find Olivia in her office. Or the English lounge. Or the library.

What I did find was a series of not-so-subtle glances from other faculty and a very awkward encounter with another teaching assistant, who looked like she wanted to ask if I needed an alibi.

I ended up outside the Humanities building, leaning against a brick pillar, and texting her with shaking fingers.

Hey. Can we talk? I just heard about the board meeting.

No response.

I typed again.

I didn't know they dragged you into it. I'm so sorry.

Still nothing.

My chest felt like it was being sat on by the full weight of campus bureaucracy and every judgmental whisper.

Was this my fault?

Was this just some stupid, slow-motion disaster that I'd pulled her into without thinking?

I had feelings. Real ones. And I never once wanted to put her in a position like this. But the truth was, Olivia Sinclair was the first person who made me feel like I wasn't just surviving college. I was becoming someone in it. And I couldn't stand the thought that I might be the reason she lost her standing, her respect, her reputation, over this mess.

That night, I walked past the English Department and found one of the flyers Benjamin had made for a department mixer. The theme?

"Shakespeare in the Courtyard: Sonnets, Cider, and Mild Scandal."

I wanted to laugh and scream at the same time.

As life would have it the next day, I got called in by Benjamin to visit his office.

As I entered Benjamin's office, I find Professor Mayer, the head of the Creative Writing track I'd just transferred into sitting there.

"Ethan," she said, motioning me to sit.

"I will leave you two alone," Benjamin said and leaves his office and closes the door behind him.

"What's going on?"

"I wanted to talk with you, not as an administrator, but as someone who knows what it's like to have a dazzling light shining directly on your personal life."

I sat. Quiet. Suspicious.

She folded her hands. "This is a difficult position you're in. And from what I gather, you didn't ask for the attention."

"No, ma'am."

"But it's here, nonetheless. So, the question becomes: how do you protect the people around you?"

That hit.

Hard.

Because I knew she wasn't just talking about me anymore.

"She did nothing wrong," I said, voice low. "And the only thing she's guilty of is being decent to me. Kind."

"I believe you," Mayer said. "But sometimes, institutions don't care about what's true. They care about what's clean."

I swallowed. "What should I do?"

She looked me straight in the eye.

"Decide what matters more. Your image or your integrity. Then act accordingly. Quietly. Thoughtfully. And above all. Don't make this worse for her. Remember, you only have this one test next Wednesday and if you pass it, you graduate."

I walked out of there with one thought in mind: Olivia Sinclair.

She needed to know everything, but first I needed to help clean up the mess I caused.

That night, I deleted every public post I'd ever made that even hinted at Olivia.

I didn't stop caring. I didn't stop feeling.

But I will stop feeding the fire.

Because if the board wanted a clean story, they weren't getting one from me.

They'd get something real—or nothing at all.

20

It is Real

The board meeting had left a heaviness in my chest that clung like storm clouds. I'd walked out of that room feeling like I was carrying a secret on my back with the weight of a scandal pinned to it. They had said nothing definitive. No formal accusations, no disciplinary action. But the way they looked at me?

It was enough.

Enough to make me question every boundary I thought I had carefully maintained.

Enough to make me question him.

And yet I hadn't stopped thinking about Ethan. Not once.

The hotel. The kiss. The Shakespearean karaoke. His voice cracking slightly as he sang a ballad with all the misplaced confidence of a drunk nobleman. The way he looked at me like I was an entire galaxy instead of a professor with cracked edges and a grieving past.

So, when I finally saw his name light up my phone a few days later, his words hesitant and apologetic, my thumb hovered over the keyboard for a full ten minutes before I wrote:

Come over. Please. Tonight. Let's talk.

It was just past 11 when I heard the knock.

Soft. Hesitant.

I opened the door to find him standing there, hoodie half-zipped, hands in his pockets, hair slightly damp like he'd run his fingers through it a dozen times on the walk over.

"Hey," he said, like we hadn't nearly imploded our entire lives in a hotel room two weeks ago.

"Come in," I said gently.

I led him inside. The lights were low, with only a warm lamp by the couch and the amber flicker of a candle that smelled faintly of cinnamon and cedar. I had cleaned little. I hadn't tried to stage the space. This wasn't for appearances. This was real.

He stood awkwardly in the middle of my living room, eyes tracing the spines of books, the framed photo of Micah on the bookshelf, the worn throw blanket I draped in during office hours when the heating had gone out.

"You're safe here," I said.

He looked up at that. And his eyes showed all that ache. All that love he hadn't said aloud yet.

"I never wanted to hurt you," he whispered. "Or make your job harder. I swear I didn't think any of this would go as far as it did."

I stepped closer. "Neither did I."

"I didn't mean to fall for you like this," he admitted, voice raw. "But I did. I have. And I'm not sorry."

That undid me.

My hand reached for his before I even fully realised I was doing it.

"Ethan."

He looked at me like I was holding his entire world in my hands. Maybe I was.

"I've been scared," I said, the words falling out faster now. "Not just of the board. Not just of the lines we've crossed or the ones we danced around, but of this. Of how you make me feel, like I'm still allowed to want something for myself."

His grip tightened. "You are. You're allowed to want joy. And love. And something messy and real."

I smiled, eyes stinging. "Even if that joy is a slightly emotionally disastrous student who quotes Shakespeare at karaoke?"

He grinned, stepping closer. "Especially if it's that."

And then there was nothing else left between us.

No classroom. No titles. No whispered rumours or faculty expectations.

Just warmth. Just breath. Just the slow, hesitant brush of his lips on mine asking for permission.

I gave it.

With both hands, both lips, and the soft gasp of surrender that escaped from my throat when I melted into him.

The kiss wasn't wild or rushed.

It was slow.

Reverent.

The kind of kiss you give when you've waited so long to be allowed to feel something that matters.

He kissed my cheek. My temple. The corner of my mouth.

I rested my forehead against his. "This isn't simple."

"No," he whispered. "But it's us."

I led him to my bedroom, and we undressed.

There was a reverence in his eyes as he looked at me undress. A tenderness that made me feel cherished, seen in a way that went beyond the physical. It was as if he were holding something precious, something fragile, and the care he took with me mirrored that feeling.

He reached over to me and his hands traced the curve of my back; a soft sigh escaped my lips. It wasn't a sigh of passion, not yet, but one of pure comfort, like sinking into a warm bath after a long day. Each touch was feather light, a gentle exploration rather than a demanding caress. My breath hitched slightly as his fingers brushed against my neck, sending a shiver that wasn't born of cold.

A warmth bloomed in my chest, as he gently laid beside me, building once again my anticipation with each soft kiss he pressed against my forehead, my cheek, my breasts. It wasn't a frantic desire, but a slow, unfolding pleasure, a sense of being utterly safe and completely desired in this gentle way. My own hands, resting on his head as he slowly navigated himself to that most moist of places in me, giving him a silent invitation for him to continue this tender dance.

In this moment, it wasn't just about the physical but about the profound connection we were sharing, a language spoken without words, only through the softest of touches and the most loving of gazes.

He was in me so beautifully that I cried. Silent tears of joy, for it had been so long since a man had made love to me this way. It took what seemed to be an eternity of pleasure for me to climax and then to feel him sharing himself in me.

Ethan leaned to the right and closed his eyes, but his hands kept caressing my arm, stroking it gently as if by tracing his fingers on my arm he could continue to feel me.

We fell asleep in each other arms shortly afterwards.

I woke up at 3AM to an empty bed. Ethan was gone, but I heard noises outside.

I grabbed my robe and saw him sitting on the couch, and I sat next to him, my legs tangled around his like we'd been here a hundred times before. He took my hand. My head is on his chest. Silence stretching long and comfortable between us.

"I changed my major," he said eventually, his voice a gentle rumble against my ear. "I'm graduating sooner."

I looked up at him. "Why?"

"Because I want to meet you halfway," he said. "Not as your student. Not as a footnote. But as a man who loves you and wants to build something that isn't hidden."

My heart cracked open.

And all I could say was, "Okay."

Then softer: "Me too."

Just like that.

No promises.

No dramatic declarations.

One thing I knew was that whatever this was.

It is real.

Next thing I knew, we were asleep again in each other's arms.

21

Expunged

I stared at the screen, reading the email for a full minute before it hit me.

"You have successfully completed all program requirements. You are eligible to graduate."

I blinked. Once. Twice.

I rubbed my eyes like I was trying to exorcise a ghost.

Done. I was actually done.

No more student ID. No more semester plans. No more office hours or borrowed textbooks. I was free.

And suddenly, the air around me felt very different.

Which meant so did everything with Olivia.

I paced the apartment, phone in hand, chewing the inside of my cheek like a caffeinated chihuahua. Then, before I could overthink it, I called her.

"Ethan?" she answered, her voice warm and surprised.

"Hey," I said, trying not to sound like I was vibrating with nervous energy. "I got the notification. I'm officially eligible to graduate. No strings. No classes left."

Silence. Then a breathy, stunned, "How wonderful. You did it?"

"I did it," I confirmed, a smile spreading across my face. "And I want us to meet with the board."

She hesitated. "Ethan..."

"No, hear me out. I want to go in. I want us to go in. Tell them everything. Not the scandalised version, my version. Our version. We've danced around this long enough. Let's just clear the air. On our terms."

There was a pause, then, quietly, "Okay. I'll set it up."

Three days later, I walked into the boardroom like a man walking into a court case he didn't fully understand but was fully committed to winning with sheer gumption and a good pair of boots.

Long table. Half the faculty board dressed like this was a deposition and not just a Tuesday. Olivia was already there and was sitting at the far end, cool and composed, but her eyes met mine as I entered. A soft flicker. Encouragement.

"Mr Carter," Dean Wexler said with a vaguely disapproving nod. "Thank you for coming. We understand you requested this meeting?"

"I did," I said, sliding into the seat next to Olivia like I belonged there. "And thank you for making time. I promise this won't be boring."

One of the board members raised a sceptical eyebrow. Another adjusted her glasses like she was preparing to make notes on my eventual sentencing.

"I'm here," I said clearly, "to talk about the rumours. The elephant in the room. The extremely persistent narrative that there's something inappropriate going on between myself and Professor Sinclair."

Murmurs rippled around the table. Olivia's posture tightened.

"Well," said Professor Price from history, "is there?"

I gave a sheepish smile.

"That depends. Are we talking 'inappropriate' by academic standards or by Victorian ones? Because if it's the latter, I regret to inform you, I once saw Professor Sinclair's ankle."

More murmurs.

Someone choked on their coffee.

Olivia covered her face briefly with her hand.

"Let me be clear," I said, tone shifting slightly. "I never took advantage of my position as a student. There was never coercion, never favouritism, no grades influenced, no lines crossed while I was her student and teaching assistant. Professor Sinclair is a professional educator and far more cautious than I ever was. Which, frankly, was frustrating at the time. But in hindsight? Incredibly respectable."

Dean Wexler leaned forward. "You admit there were feelings?"

"Absolutely," I said. "But not ones born from infatuation or rebellion. We connected. Over literature, over loss, over late-night karaoke that I deeply regret but would do again in a heartbeat."

A laugh escaped someone near the back.

"I'm not asking for anyone's blessing," I added. "I just want you to hear it from me. I'm no longer a student. I'm a graduate. And if I have anything to say about it, Olivia, Professor Sinclair, won't be remembered for some rumour. She'll be remembered as the reason I made it through. With my head on, and my heart still open."

Olivia stared at me like I'd just recited Shakespeare again, but this time with less tequila and more sincerity.

The board went quiet. Which was never a good sign.

Then Associate Provost Heller leaned back and said, "You know, I always thought the scandal would come from the chem department. All those open flames."

Laughter broke the tension. Olivia exhaled. Dean Wexler glanced down at his notes.

"Well," he said, "this is certainly a new frontier. But, given your graduation status, and provided Professor Sinclair maintains her professional standards..."

"She always has," I cut in.

"—then the board has no grounds for a disciplinary action at this time."

I add.

"Just a second Dean Wexler. I have two conditions First, there will be no disciplinary action by the board to take. As a matter of fact, you will remove the previous note on her record and second, I believe Professor Daniels is retiring later this year, and you will need to replace his position. I want you to nominate and approve Professor Benjamin Harper as his replacement. If not, I will have no choice but to release several highly classified documents I have in my possession concerning two board members."

The room burst into chaos.

"Everyone! Calm down please," shouted Dean Wexler.

When the room settled, Dean Wexler looked around and saw a few worried faces, then just said: "Done. No need for more agitation here. All remarks and notes will be expunged from Professor Sinclair's record, and Professor Harper will join the board. Is that it, Mr Carter?"

Relief flooded my chest.

"That is all, yes Dean."

Olivia looked like she'd just released a breath she'd been holding for a decade.

"However," he added, eyes narrowing, "I recommend you keep your karaoke performances strictly off-campus."

I nodded solemnly. "With every fibre of my being, sir."

As we left the boardroom, Olivia walked beside me in silence for a moment before saying, "You just Shakespeare-mansplained your way through an academic tribunal."

I grinned. "It worked, didn't it?"

She stopped, turned to me, and took my hand. "It did."

"By the way, Mr Carter, what sensitive information were you going to expose?"

"Nothing. I just bluffed. I figure someone in that room had a secret."

Then she kissed me. Right there in the empty hallway.

Soft. Certain.

And entirely earned.

22

The Offer

The email arrived on a Thursday.

Of course it did.

Thursdays had always been suspiciously eventful in Olivia's life.

The day she got hired at the university, the day Micah's last letter had arrived from Afghanistan, and now this. She stared at the subject line like it was a mirage.

"Congratulations! You've been selected for the Global Fellowship in Comparative Literature - University of Edinburgh."

She re-read it five times, blinking, mouth slightly agape. The fellowship had been a long shot. A dreamy, distant idea she'd submitted a proposal for six months ago and then promptly buried under a mountain of essays and recommendation letters. It was prestigious, intensely competitive, and just the kind of once-in-a-decade opportunity she'd assumed was meant for someone else.

But it wasn't.

It was for her.

She clutched her phone, fingers trembling slightly, and before she could spiral into analysis-paralysis, she dialled Ethan at the pub.

He answered on the first ring. "Hey, what's up? You, okay?"

There was no preamble. "I got the Edinburgh fellowship."

Pause. Then, in his classic Ethan way, he whispered dramatically, "We're moving to Scotland?!"

Olivia blinked. "I didn't say I was going to move."

"But you are going to move. You must go," he interrupted. "You earned it. It's huge. Come on, Professor Sinclair, you can't just drop a bomb like that and expect me to play it cool."

She sat down, dazed. "It's for a year. Maybe two."

"Even better. I've been dying to wear tweed unironically."

She laughed, the tension breaking in her chest. "Ethan, your studies. Your job?"

"I'm serious," he said gently. "Go. I'll come with you."

That stopped her cold. "What?"

"Yeah," he said. "I looked into some master's programs. There's a few at Edinburgh. Lit. Journalism. Creative writing.

They all accept mid-year applicants. I can apply. And we can do this. Together. Besides, I can work at a pub there just like I can work at one here."

Olivia stared at her reflection on the dark screen of her laptop. "You'd really do that? Leave your friends, your home, everything for me?"

"You changed your life for your students every damn day. Let me change mine for once."

By July, they were on a plane.

It was an absurdly romantic, stupidly chaotic move.

Ethan got accepted into the university's Master of Arts in Creative Writing program. Olivia submitted her official acceptance to the Global Fellowship. They sublet a tiny, ancient-looking flat in Old Town Edinburgh that had a fireplace with questionable functionality and a kitchen barely large enough for one person to turn around in.

And they were happy.

Mostly.

"Where's my scarf? The good one? The one with the little moth holes I pretend are fashion statements?" Olivia hollered from the bedroom.

Ethan, half-buried under a pile of manuscript drafts and used coffee mugs, called back, "The one that smells like regret and lavender? Check the coat rack."

"If you're going to insult my scarf," she said, appearing in the doorway, hair wild, and cheeks flushed, "at least help me find it."

He stood up with exaggerated effort. "I can't feel my legs. I've been sitting cross-legged since 6 a.m. editing my workshop story."

She grinned. "Is this what domestic life is like now? Literary arguments and coffee stains?"

He walked over, pulled her close by the waist. "I wouldn't trade it. Not even for a New York Times Best Seller."

Olivia kissed his nose. "You say that now. Wait until you read my fellowship lecture on the semiotics of desire in Victorian ghost stories."

"Damn, I am getting hot just with the title," he murmured.

"You have a problem," she laughed, and they stood there for a beat, just breathing together.

Edinburgh suited Olivia in the strangest, most surprising ways. The grey skies, the gothic architecture, the hum of ancient history on the cobblestones. Her lectures were well received. Students hung on her words. One even brought her a home-baked shortbread shaped like a Brontë novel.

Ethan flourished, too. His workshop classmates found him both infuriatingly charismatic and annoyingly talented.

His professor kept writing "Too charming. Make it worse for your characters."

One rainy afternoon, Olivia found him at the university library, squinting over a notepad.

"You look constipated," she said, dropping into the seat beside him.

He didn't look up. "I wrote a love poem and now I hate it."

"That's the writerliest sentence I've ever heard."

"Want to read it?"

She leaned in. "Only if I can mock the metaphors."

He handed it over.

She read it.

And fell a little more in love. Not because it was perfect. But because it wasn't. Because it was raw and flawed and filled with him.

But it wasn't all sunshine and metaphor.

There were fights.

Small ones.

Medium ones.

The occasional large one that ended with someone stomping off into the cold, dramatic Scottish mist.

Like the time Ethan lost his passport. On a weekend trip to the Highlands. During a tour of a distillery.

"You lost it where?!" Olivia shrieked, standing in the parking lot while Ethan patted his coat for the fifth time.

"I think the goat ate it."

"You absolute maniac."

Or the time Olivia forgot their anniversary because she was too buried in prepping her keynote address.

Ethan left a passive-aggressive post-it on the fridge that read: "Happy One Year Since You Forgot You Like Me."

They laughed later.

After pizza.

After apologies.

After making love.

Then, one December evening, everything stilled.

They were at the Christmas market.

Lights strung between booths. The smell of roasted chestnuts and mulled wine filling the air. Olivia wore her moth-eaten scarf. Ethan had a tartan beanie that made him look like a very lost tourist.

"I got you something," he said, pulling a small box from his coat.

"We said no gifts," she protested.

"I lied," he said, handing it over.

She opened it. Inside, a necklace. Simple. A silver quill. Symbolic and cheesy and perfect.

"It's beautiful," she whispered.

He tucked a strand of hair behind her ear. "You're the reason I write now. Not just for grades. Not for professors. For the first time, I write for me. For us."

She kissed him.

Under the lights.

In front of a booth selling novelty whisky hats.

And she thought yes. This. This is what love looks like now.

They made it through the year. And then another.

Olivia published her first book on Gothic feminism in British literature.

Ethan landed a short story in a major literary journal and started his novel.

They never officially planned what came next.

But one afternoon, lying on their tiny sofa with her head on his chest and his hand stroking her hair, Olivia murmured, "We should stay. At least a little longer."

"You read my mind," Ethan said.

They had each other.

The books.

The bad karaoke.

And Edinburgh.

What more could they need?

Well, maybe one goat-free trip to the Highlands.

But that could wait since Ethan looks at me, smiles and says: "Let's get married!"

Acknowledgements

I would like to acknowledge two wonderful authors that have allowed me to reference their books in this novel. I have read and reviewed their novels and found them a great read.

Please visit Greg Mutton's website to purchase his books.

https://books.by/greg-mutton-author

Please visit Deen Ferrell's website to purchase his books.

https://www.deenferrell.com/

Reviews

https://worldbookreviews.com.au/greg-mutton/

https://worldbookreviews.com.au/deen-ferrell/

About The Author

Flung into one of life's most daunting challenges at just 11 years old, José's journey began in Havana, Cuba. The Cuban Revolution uprooted his family, forcing his parents to make a heart-wrenching decision: send him away, alone, to safety. José boarded a plane, uncertain of what lay ahead, and landed not in the comfort of familiar faces but at an orphanage in a small Georgia town called Washington.

For the next seven years, he navigated life as a stranger in a foreign land. Letters were few, and the hope of reuniting with his parents became a distant dream.

Finally, at 18—now a high school graduate in Atlanta—he embraced his family once again. The reunion was bittersweet, for José had grown up without them, becoming independent far sooner than most.

Determined to carve out a life for himself, José pursued a degree in Business Administration at Georgia State University. He stepped into the world of finance, starting at First National Bank of Atlanta (now Wells Fargo). His natural talent for numbers and strategic thinking propelled him to become a project manager in financial consulting, leading to high-stakes ventures. His career took him across the globe, from bustling cities in the United States to financial hubs in Europe and even the sunburnt coasts of Australia.

It was in Camden, New South Wales, that a new chapter of José's life began. While exploring the quiet rhythms of this Australian town, José stumbled upon a local writers' group. What began as a casual interest soon grew into an unquenchable passion. The stories swirling in his mind took shape, and from that creative spark, Danny Monk, his first major character, was born—a mischievous, intriguing figure who captured the complexities José had observed throughout his life. Writing Danny's story was a revelation, and with that, José discovered a new calling.

Fast forward to today. José is not just a writer but a prolific storyteller, balancing multiple projects at once. He is deep into his seventh short story collection while simultaneously crafting his latest work—a crime novel slated for release in 2026. His books, filled with engaging characters and complex narratives, reflect a life rich with experiences, challenges, and triumphs.

Yet José's world is not confined to the keyboard and screen. Inspiration comes from everywhere, and one of his favourite pastimes is to wander the local mall, quietly observing people, noting quirks, behaviours, and snippets of conversation that might spark a new character or plot twist. When he's not writing or gathering ideas, José immerses himself in literature, feeding his mind with the words of others.

Outside of his creative pursuits, José treasures the simple pleasures of life—particularly long walks with his wife, Miriam, through the scenic streets of Spring Farm. Their leisurely strolls are a cherished routine; moments of reflection where stories, memories, and dreams intertwine.

José's life is a tapestry woven from adversity, perseverance, and creativity. From the orphanage in Georgia to the financial districts of the world, and now to the quiet corners of Spring Farm, where stories are born, his journey is a testament to the resilience of the human spirit. And with each book he writes, José not only tells stories but also leaves behind pieces of himself, enriching the lives of readers across the globe.

José F. Nodar © 2025

Other books by José F. Nodar

English

- Books, Pens & Larceny
- Mending Hearts at Crystal Cove
- A Love Finally Spoken
- The Legacy Compass
- The Universe Between Us
- The Time Bus
- SEX
- Stories to Share with My Partner Book 1
- Stories to Share with My Partner Book 2
- Stories to Share with My Partner Book 3
- Stories to Share with My Partner Book 4
- Stories to Share with My Partner Book 5
- Stories to Share with My Partner Book 6
- Stories to Share with My Partner Book 7
- Stories to Share with My Partner Book 8
- Stories to Share with My Partner Book 9

Spanish

- Cuentos Para Compartir con Mi Pareja Libro 1
- Cuentos Para Compartir con Mi Pareja Libro 2
- Cuentos Para Compartir con Mi Pareja Libro 3
- Libros, Bolígrafos y Hurto
- Reparando Corazones en Crystal Cove
- Un Amor Expresado
- El Autobús del Tiempo